DUMP DAYS

OTHER YEARLING BOOKS YOU WILL ENJOY:

YEARLING BOOKS/YOUNG YEARLINGS/YEARLING CLASSICS are designed especially to entertain and enlighten young people. Patricia Reilly Giff, consultant to this series, received her bachelor's degree from Marymount College and a master's degree in history from St. John's University. She holds a Professional Diploma in Reading and a Doctorate of Humane Letters from Hofstra University. She was a teacher and reading consultant for many years, and is the author of numerous books for young readers.

For a complete listing of all Yearling titles,
write to Dell Readers Service,
P.O. Box 1045, South Holland, IL 60473.

DUMP DAYS

Jerry Spinelli

A Yearling Book

Published by
Dell Publishing
a division of
Bantam Doubleday Dell Publishing Group, Inc.
666 Fifth Avenue
New York, New York 10103

The characters and events portrayed in this book are fictitious. Any similarities to real persons, living or dead, are coincidental and not intended by the author.

The trademark Yearling® is registered in the U.S. Patent and Trademark Office.

The trademark Dell® is registered in the U.S. Patent and Trademark Office.

ISBN: 0-440-40421-5

Reprinted by arrangement with Little, Brown and Company, Inc.

Printed in the United States of America

June 1991

10 9 8 7 6 5 4 3

OPM

For Margaret and Andrew Roy

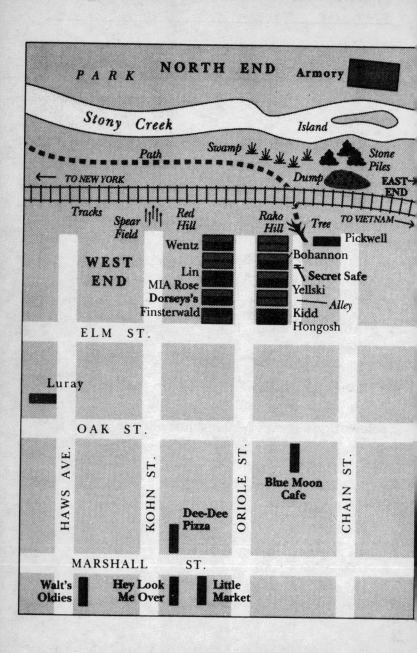

1

"Ahhhh . . . man."

"You said it."

"This is the life."

"Don't get no better."

We were stretched out over all four steps, the soles of our sneaks hanging just an inch above the sidewalk. The concrete felt a little rough on my forearm, like a cat's tongue, and cool.

"Yeah . . . this is it."

"*It,* baby."

We stretched out some more. Enjoying it.

Me and Duke.

I said, "Got your cards?"

He said, "You see 'em?"

"Why don't you go get them?"

"Don't feel like it." .

"How many you got now?"

"Don't know. You?"

"Two hundred and fifty-six. You gotta know how many Roses you got."

"Three."

"Five, baby."

Pete Rose baseball cards are just about the most valuable things you can have.

"You weren't so chicken to flip," he said, "I'd win them Roses from ya."

"Who's chicken?"

"Wanna flip?"

"Any time."

"Now."

"Right now? Go get 'em."

He sat up straight. "Let's go."

I slouched back. "Forget it, man. I ain't going nowhere. I'm here to relax."

He sat back. "Later."

"Yeah."

"Tomorrow."

"Right."

We sat some more.

I said, "Know something?"

"What?"

"Nah. Can't say it. Sounds crazy."

"Say it."

"Well, y'know, this is the first day of vacation and all?"

"First *hour*."

"Yeah, right. Well. It sounds crazy, but I can't believe it's ever gonna end. I mean, I *know* it will, in my head. But I don't *believe* it. I believe it's gonna last forever. Crazy, huh?"

He nodded. He knew.

I said, "Got your knife?"

He fished it out of his pocket, handed it over. Swiss Army knife. I opened up the different parts. Thirteen of them, including even a little fork and a spoon. He eats with it — at home, in restaurants, everywhere. He always has it with him. Nine out of ten problems Duke has, he can handle with the knife.

I folded up the knife, gave it back. "Saw one in a magazine."

"Yeah?"

"Yeah. Had fifty things."

"Keep dreamin'."

"I ain't lying. It showed a picture. Some of the things, when you fold them out, *they* got things that fold out."

"Fifty . . ." He whistled. "Man. You could do anything."

"All you'd ever need. And a bike."

"Be set for life."

We thought about it.

After a while I got up, moseyed out to the curb,

kicked a stone across the street. It hopped the other curb and knocked up against Finsterwald's steps. I froze.

"Way to go, Einstein," Duke hissed.

We both held our breath, praying Finsterwald didn't hear, wasn't lurking behind one of the dark green, pulled-down shades. Finsterwald hated kids — maybe all kinds of people — but especially kid people. There's a legend that he caught a kid in his backyard once, chasing a ball, and the kid — now he's a man — is up in the state hospital ever since. Nobody ever, ever sits on Finsterwald's steps.

Soon as I could make myself move, I got back to the steps. I wanted to talk about something, anything but Finsterwald. "What're you thinking?" I said.

Duke didn't answer for a while. Then: "A zep."

"Really? In the morning?"

"Yeah. Can't help it."

Spit came trickling under my tongue. "Uh-oh . . . I think I'm getting it too."

"Close your eyes," he said. His were already closed. "You see it?"

"Wait . . . yep . . . there it is."

"Can't be peppers on yours."

"Nope. But yours got 'em."

"Right."

Anywhere else, it might be called a hoagie, or a sub, or a hero. In Two Mills it's a zep. And even though at first it might look like the others, it's not. Like, you'll never find lettuce on a zep. Or mayonnaise.

10

The zep was invented in Two Mills in 1938, and down through the ages they've all been exactly alike: Italian salami, provolone cheese, tomatoes, onions, oregano, and oil. On a roll from Morabito's bakery. The tomato slices are always thick, deep red, and juicy, and the onions are pearly white Bermudas — the kind you could take a whole bite out of without crying. You just say, "Gimme a zep." About hot peppers, you don't wait to be asked. You just add, "peppers," or, if you're like me, "no peppers."

"Man," I said, "I'm *tasting* mine."

"Tasting?" he sneered. "Shoot, I'm already on my *second* one."

For a long time we sat there with our zeps.

My eyes shot open as Duke jumped down from the steps, out to the middle of the street, turned. He was making two fists. He looked in pain.

"I gotta have one."

"Now?"

"Pretty soon."

"Lou's?"

He came to the curb. "Yeah."

Lou's is where the best zeps are. It's way down the East End.

"Know what else?" he said.

"What?"

"To go with the zep, strawberry milk."

"Dig it."

He came back to the steps, sat down. "Whole quarta strawberry milk for this dude."

"You got it."

"Yeah."

We high-fived and leaned back again.

"And for me —" I said.

"Yeah?"

"Marcy's, baby!"

"All riiight! Yeah!"

High five.

Marcy's means Marcy's Water Ice. The world's best. Homemade right there. You don't have to wait for it to get slushy-drinky. It already is.

"Lemon," I said.

"Root beer," he said.

Lemon's the best. So good you can feel the pulp in your mouth.

"Tell ya, though," he said.

"What?"

"You know when it's best, don'tcha?"

"Yeah, when it's in your mouth."

"When you're sweating. When the sweat's pouring off you like bacon grease, man. That's when you want it. That's when you'd let them leave you back one year just for a Marcy's."

He was right.

"Okay," I said, "we gotta do something to work up the sweat. Ride somewhere?"

We thought.

Duke said, "Singing Bridge."

I punched his knee. "Perfect!"

The Singing Bridge. Up near Valley Forge. It goes

12

over the Schuylkill, and it's only wide enough for one lane, and the bottom of it is a steel grating, so you can look right down through it to the river, and your tires make a kind of hummy-singy sound when you ride across. The best thing to do is wait in front of the bridge till you spot a big truck coming, then you jump onto the bridge in front of it. What happens is, you hold up the truck because he can't pass you, and you know he's not going to run you over, but still, it's a little scary, because you're not sure if *he* knows he's not going to run you over, and so you pedal like mad so he couldn't catch you even if he wanted to, and the faster you go the higher the bridge sings. When you veer off on the other side, if you're not sweating, you never will be.

"And after all that," I said, "we could use some rest, too."

"Peace and quiet."

"Nice and cool."

"Dark."

"Movies!"

"Wednesday matinee, baby!"

High fives!

We settled back. Relaxing. But excited, too.

I said, "Know what we got here?"

"More'n a zep."

"Or a Marcy's."

We stared at each other. The idea and the word came to me at the same time: "A *day*."

For a minute nobody said anything. Suddenly Duke

jumped down in front of the steps, facing me. "You ready for this?" His mouth was part sneer, part grin. His finger was pointing straight at my nose. "*The. Per. Fect. Day.*"

We gaped at each other. We knew we had stumbled onto something big. I got the shivers.

Then: "What in the name of —"

My mother's voice. From above. Duke looked up, moved. "Hi, Mrs. Kidd." His answer was the window screen scraping open. I leaned back, looked straight up, and there was my mother's face coming out of the bedroom window, like a cuckoo. No words. Just staring straight down at me with that squinty, bamboozled look I get a lot, like she just came out of a coma to find herself two million years into the future.

She squeezed her eyes shut, hoping I would disappear. She opened them. I was still there. She said, "I thought I was dreaming."

She looked like she expected an answer from me. I didn't give her any. What are you supposed to say to that?

She said — whispered, actually, "You know what time it is?"

I didn't have a watch on. How did I know?

She said, "It is exactly ten minutes after six in the morning. Your father isn't even up for work yet. Now get in here, or get off the steps."

Her face went back in. The screen scraped down.

2

We moseyed on down the street. The block I live on is the last block on Oriole, and that's the best kind of block there is: a dead end. Because you don't just get more street in both directions. In one direction you do, but in the other you get, well, in the case of Oriole, all kinds of neat stuff: the tracks, the dump, the stone piles, the woods, the path, the creek, the hills. A dead end's not the end of things, it's the beginning.

The houses on Oriole Street are brick row houses, some with skinny alleyways between. Front steps, no porches. Not too fancy, but great for bouncing tennis balls off of. The builders must have had a lot of bricks left over — the sidewalks are brick too.

Duke parked himself on one of the steps. To an outsider, all the row houses would look pretty much alike. Not to us. This one was the Bohannons'.

I slid in alongside him, lounged back. Duke had a faraway look, semi-grinning. The idea that he had said — *perfect day* — bobbed in the air between us. It was so neat, so new, almost holy. I was afraid to spoil it by loading words on it, or even thinking about it too much.

The doorknob jiggled behind us. We straightened up, turned. The knob kept making noises. The door opened, and there stood Erin Bohannon, all four-years-old, three-feet-tall of her. Grinning ear to ear. Naked. Not a stitch. Mile-wide-grinning down at us.

Then, behind her, a voice, woman's — but no words, just muffled sounds, like if your mouth was gagged and you were trying to yell. "*Mm*-mm! . . . Mm-*mm!*"

In a flash of tiny white hiney, Erin was past us, off the steps, yelping like a house dog let loose. Then Mrs. Bohannon, looming in the doorway above us, tying her bathrobe, her cheeks ballooning, her wide eyes darting wildly, her head cocked back, snapping forward, a green stream of mouthwash shooting to the sidewalk beside the steps. A deep huffy intake of breath: "Er-*rinn!*"

Erin was stopped in front of the Zavinskis' Volkswagen, about five houses down, facing us, yelping, "Yippee!" and jumping up and down with both feet.

By now me and Duke were standing down from the steps, off to the side, to give Mrs. Bohannon all the room she needed. But that's not how it happened. She said, "Fellas, please" — the "please" came out full of breath — "would you please go get her for me? Would you please?" There was a faint minty smell.

"Sure," we both said, no-sweat-style; like, Hey, we do this every day. Erin saw us heading her way — just what she wanted. She started jumping like a lunatic, like the sidewalk was a loose lid, and she had to stomp it shut.

I whispered to Duke, "What're we gonna do?"

"Catch her."

"How?"

"Herd her and nab her."

"I'll herd," I said, "you nab."

Seeing a naked girl, that was nothing new. Duke has six sisters besides his four brothers, and I have my little six-year-old sister, Bertie. And Erin Bohannon takes her clothes off whenever she gets the chance, as long as it's warm enough. But nobody ever said to catch her before.

When we got about two houses from her, she bolted for the dead end.

"The tracks!" shrieked Mrs. Bohannon.

Duke was already firing out, but Erin was quicker. She shot between two cars and into the street, her mother shrieking, "Cars!"

Duke stationed himself at the dead end end of the street, me at the other. She just kept going nutso, stomping, flapping, careening in circles. Duke motioned for me to move, drive her toward him. I spread my arms and started inching forward. Once, she tried to dart past me, but I jumped in front and turned her back. She laughed. She loved it. Then she darted over to a telephone pole and hid behind it. "Can't see me-eee," she called.

She was right. We closed in. Even just a couple feet away, I still couldn't see her. Suddenly — *bam!* — there she was — "Boo!" — leaping at me, dashing past, me reaching out, no time to think, grabbing her — *caught!* Little bare white fish squirming in my hand.

I picked her up by her shoulders — no bigger than golf balls — and held her out to Duke at arms' length. "Here."

Duke chuckled, took her, hoisted her to his shoulders. She rode him calling, "Hi, Mom-meee!" back to her house.

As Erin ran squealing inside, Mrs. Bohannon dug some change out of her robe pocket and handed it to Duke — "Thank you, fellas" — and shut the door.

"How much?" I said.

Duke looked. "Fifty." He gave me a quarter.

We were ready to re-park on the Bohannons' steps, but I couldn't stand the thought of Erin escaping again. "Let's check out the dump," I said.

3

"Ratball?" said Duke.

"Yeah, sure," I said.

The sun was squatting on the East End. It was already bright enough to snag itself on a couple points in the dump. You'd get excited, seeing the little pin-flash, the star-wink, and then you take another step or two, and all it was, was a chewing gum wrapper or the rim of a tin can.

That's dumps: they keep teasing you. That football there — looks perfect, right? Fudge-brown, pebbly skin, Chiclety white laces. You reach in, poke it with a stick — it caves in like a rotten fruit. Turn it over — a puncture you could jam your fist through. That badminton racket — you work the thin end of a branch into one of the string holes and lift — the head of the racket comes up, the handle stays.

I believe in the Dump Fairy. He comes in the night and arranges everything so the good side is showing. You know it, but you still keep coming back. Looking. Hoping.

Duke got the old snow shovel from the hiding place. I found a stick. We were moseying along the edge of the dump, looking — not for rats yet, just for stuff, something new, since last time we looked.

I said, "Roller skating. At the rink. After the movies."

He nodded. "Then Ramjets."

I punched his shoulder. "Yeah!" Ramjets. Video game in the back of Dee-Dee Pizza. "For a half-hour straight."

He sneered. "Shoot. An hour."

Something caught my eye. "There!"

He looked, shook his head. "Doll head."

Another step, I saw he was right. Smooth, flesh-colored bald back of a doll's head. I had thought ball. Duke is quick and always right. He knows his junk. Not only does he live next to a dump, but his father goes around in his pickup, scavenging streets on the night before their trash collection days. Says he got the idea in Vietnam, where he was for the war. Says they don't waste anything over there. Sometimes Duke goes along.

"Walt's," I said. Walt's Oldies. Look through the old comic books. Tons.

Duke started laughing.

"What?" I said.

"Buy one."

I laughed. "For once."

"Buy five. Each of us."

"Give him a heart attack!"

Duke said, "Okay . . . okay . . ." whispering, patting the air with his hand. (Spook the rats too much and they won't come out for an hour.)

The Perfect Day.

I poked him, whispered, "Y'know the problem, don'tcha?"

"What?"

"Money."

He stepped into the dump. "Ain't no problem."

The dump was, maybe, the size of a Little League infield. Sort of round. A big hole with trash. Duke Pickwell, the only person I know who would walk with rats, eased himself down into it. About ten feet in he stopped. He crouched alongside an overturned washing machine. Real slow and easy, he laid the flat, rusty face of the snow shovel in front of a sofa cushion, where stuffing was spilling out through a big gash, barfing brown cotton. He looked up, nodded.

Okay, ratball: sooner or later a rat comes strolling out onto the shovel. Duke quick flips the shovel and pitches the rat out to me. I wait till the sucker's waist-high, then — *blam!* — poleax him high and deep. Maybe over the dump. Or out to the stone piles. Or maybe all the way to the creek. Home run!

We had the shovel and stick ready five or six times since we invented the game. We were still waiting for the first rat to show.

It didn't take me long to get tired of waiting. Green- and bluebelly flies were zipping around me.

"Duke," I whisper-called. He didn't twitch. Louder: "Duke. C'mon. Let's go."

He flapped his hand: shut up and be still.

The flies were getting worse. I had never stayed still so long in my life. I wondered if my body was undergoing changes due to not moving. The flies started to sound like they were whispering: *psss-psss-psss*. I remembered I didn't take a bath the night before, yesterday being the last day of school. As if that wasn't enough, my T-shirt was brown, not to mention my hair. To those flies I was probably starting to look and smell like something that dropped out of a dinosaur. *Hey, Mabel! Lookee here! We're set fer life!*

The next noise I heard was not a fly's: "J. D.! J. D.!"

My little sister, Bertie. I turned. She was at the top of Rako Hill in her Bullwinkle nightshirt yelling to me. "J. D.! J. D.!"

I put my finger to my lips. I waved my arms.

"J. D.! You gotta come! You gotta see Mommy *now!*"

I shook my fist.

"Jay-*Deee!*"

22

Then another yell, from the dump — "Yah-hah!" — and a rat came flying through the air. I froze. The rat tumbled across the sky in a long, slow cartwheel. My only thought was, Wow! Acrobatic rat! It was all so clear — the brown rat, even its whiskers, against the blue sky. Then it was on me, on my head like a wig, four tiny feet clutching my scalp, the end of its tail kissing my lips; and just as quick, my head was free, the rat was on the ground, scooting, and then the railroad tracks were moving too, they were waving, laaazy-waving, like a pair of long, lazy silver eels . . .

"J. D. . . . J. D. . . ."

Somebody calling me, from far away. My head rocking. Slapped.

"J. D. . . . C'mon, dude, wake up . . . Wake up!"

I see Duke's face.

"Hey man, y' okay? You awake? He bite you or something?"

"Bite me . . . what? Huh?"

"The rat."

I shot to my feet. "Where is he?"

Duke got up, pointed the shovel at the dump. "There. Gone. The way you were just standing there, I thought you were gonna bunt him."

Something bothered me, something he said before. "What do you mean awake, am I awake?"

"Huh?" — he picked up a tin can — "Oh, I wanted

to know if you were outta your faint, that's" — he tossed the can into the air, walloped it: *tonnng* — "all."

I laughed. "You're crazy." He picked up another can: *tonnng*. "Cripes . . . *faint?*" I laughed louder. "Don'tcha even know what I was *doing?* Moron? When an animal's attacking you, you play possum. That's what I was doing." *Tonnng*. "Wha'd you want, me to go moving all around? So he'd bite me? You said it yourself: did he bite me. Rats carry rabies, y'know. Ever hear of rabies?" *Tonnng*. "That what I was s'pposed to do, get rabies? Huh? . . . Huh?"

He kicked a can. He looked up at Rako Hill. My sister was gone. "Your mother wants you." He headed for the hiding place to put the shovel back.

I followed. "Moron," I said.

4

Rako Hill is as steep as a hill can get and still be a hill and not a cliff. It's dirt — yellow, sparkly dirt. With gullies. If you're going to ride it, you better know the gullies. It takes guts to ride it down, calf muscles to ride up. Nobody younger than sixth grade has ever pedaled up. It's hard enough to walk up.

That's what we were doing, and it wasn't till we got to the top that we saw Bertie. She was kneeling on the ground under the gigantic tree that stands at the end of the Pickwells' backyard. Actually, you can't say the tree is at the end, since there's no fence to show exactly where the end of the Pickwells' backyard is. And maybe you can't say "yard," if you think yard means grass and flowers instead of dirt and a duck and junk piled high as the second-story windows. And maybe you can't even say "back," if that's the end of the house that all thirteen Pickwells pour in and out of.

Anyway, when Bertie saw us she popped up and ran over and plunked herself smack in our way. She had to tilt her head all the way back to look up at us. She had a watermelon-slice grin, the bottom of her Bullwinkle nightshirt was grimy, and her toes looked like they'd been dipped in chocolate. She was hiding something behind her back.

"J. D.," she grinned, "what were you doin'? Huntin' rats?"

"Yeah," I said. "What's Mom want?"

I stepped around her. She replunked herself in front of me.

"J. D. — d'juh get one?"

"No. Now c'mon, move it."

"J. D. — do you wanna" — she swung her hands in front — "*buy* one?"

She held it by the tail . . .

Duke was laughing. Howling.

"What's so funny?" I said.

"You, man, the way you jumped. D'juh pee yourself?"

"What're you talking about? You're senile." I prayed Bertie had a good grip on that tail.

Bertie started swinging it. "Don't be afraid, J. D. See, it's dead." She put on her wide-eyed, blinkycutesy face. "I'm having a special on rats today. Only one dollar."

Duke poked it with his knife. "That's not a rat, hate to tell ya."

Bertie brought it up to her face. "It's not?"

"Nope. It's a mole."

"A *mole?*" She laughed. "That's what J. D. has on his hiney!"

Duke shot me a smirky look. My face got hot.

"Moles are animals, too," Duke told her. "They live underground. Where'd you find it?"

She pointed to Duke's yard. "Over there." She examined it again. "You sure it ain't a rat?"

"Guarantee ya. Look at the nose . . . see, it's like a snout. And see, the tail's not like a rat's, not long. And the feet, see, they're used for digging."

"I thought moles were big," I said. This thing wasn't much bigger than Bertie's hand.

Duke shrugged. "I did, too. Maybe it's a baby. All I'm sayin's, that there's a mole."

Bertie grinned, all proud of herself. "A *dead* one."

Duke nodded. "Yep. Deader'n a doornail." He winked at me. "That's why you gotta hand him over."

Bertie's mouth dropped. "Huh?"

"Yep. Moles're an endangered species. It's against the law to kill one."

Bertie screeched. "I didn't kill it! It was dead when I found it!"

"Well, yeah," said Duke, looking sympathetic but

stern, "but the evidence is in your hand. You'd have a hard time proving you didn't do it in a court of law."

Bertie's sad eyes sank to the glossy black hide of the mole. Her lip quivered. "But I *didn't*. Won't they be*lieve* me?"

Duke had to look away. "Well, maybe . . . maybe not."

Uh-oh, I thought, mistake. He was giving her an opening. You can't do that with Bertie. Once you get her down, you have to kick her (so to speak). You have to forget she's only six.

Sure enough, her face perked up. "Well," she chirped, "that means they *will* believe me."

She started off. Duke reached out, grabbed her by the nightshirt. "Whoa there, pardner, you're forgetting one thing."

Bertie's head swiveled. "What's that?"

"Possession is nine-tenths of the law."

The rest of her turned. "Huh?"

"You found it *there*, right?"

"So?"

"On my property."

"So?"

"So that makes it my mole."

She glared at him for a minute. Then: "*I* didn't say that. I said I found it over" — she pointed to the other side of the alley, to the Zavinskis' backyard — "*there*. It's mine." She dangled it in front of our noses. "Wanna buy it?"

Duke bit. "How much?"

"Five dollars."

"Five dollars!" I screeched. "You said one before."

She shrugged. "That's before I knew it was a mole. Moles are five."

"Forget it."

She headed off again. Duke whispered fast. "We need it. Charge kids to see it. Make money."

I jumped out, snatched her by the nightshirt, reeled her in. She glared up at me, jammed her hand into her hip. "You ready to talk turkey?"

"Bertie," I said, "you don't need a mole. We do. We need it" — I glanced at Duke — "for our zoo."

She held it to her chest. "So? Cough up five dollars and you can have it."

"Okay, look. How about if we borrow it? Just till the zoo's over. Then you can have it back. Forever."

She looked suspicious. "You mean rent?"

I looked at Duke. "Yeah, rent. We'll rent it from you for . . . fifty cents."

"A dollar."

"Seventy-five cents."

"Two dollars."

"O-*kay!* A dollar."

She petted its head with her finger. She purred at it. "How do I know you'll take care of it?"

"Hey, we'll treat it real good," Duke told her. "We'll put it in its own little cage —"

"Her."

"Huh?"

"It's a her."

"Right. Her own little cage —"

"She doesn't *need* a cage," she snapped. "She's *dead*. How's she gonna run away?"

"Okay," he nodded, "that's cool, no problem. A box, okay? Nice little cardboard box. Put some dirt in it, make it — her — feel at home."

Bertie stomped her foot. "She don't *feel* anymore, dumbbone. This is just her body. She's decreased."

"Deceased," I said. "So, we'll rent it, okay?"

"Her."

"*Her.*"

She thought. "No."

"*What?*"

"Not for rent. You want her, you gotta buy her."

"Bertie, we don't *have* five dollars."

"Six dollars."

"What? You said five."

"That was when it was on sale. The sale's over now."

"Ber-*teeee!*"

Duke was trying not to burst out laughing.

"So," she said, like what's the problem, "put her on layaway."

"What's that?" She knows more about selling stuff than I do.

"That's when you gimme a little bit of money every week, and I promise not to sell her to *anybody* else, and then when you're *all* paid up, I hand her over to you."

Ah, now I had her. "Bertie" — I bent down to her size — "I hate to tell you this, but you don't have weeks. Remember, you said it's dead?"

She looked at it, checking. "So?"

"So, it's gonna start to rot away. Any day now. It's gonna get all stinky and smelly and fulla maggots. And germs. You don't want it. It's garbage."

Her eyes shot wide open: shock, tragedy, fury. She wheeled and stomped off.

I called: "Okay — we'll buy it! Four dollars!"

"Not for sale!"

5

When we got to my backyard gate, Bertie was standing all glum by the garbage can, my mother's arm was pointing and jabbing from the screen door, and she was commanding: "Now. . . . Now."

Bertie just stood there.

My mother's whisper is her yell. She whispered: "Now."

Bertie stomped. She lifted the lid and laid the mole, like she was putting it to bed, in the can. She glared at me.

"Put the lid back on."

She put the lid back on.

"Now come in here." My mother's arm was gone. Her voice came from the blackness behind the screen.

Bertie inched closer to the can.

"Bertie."

Bertie stomped, scowled. She hiss-whispered to me with just her lips moving over her clamped teeth, always reminds me of a mad chipmunk: "You better not touch that mole. If you do, I'll wait'll you're asleep and squirt Elmer's glue up your nose."

She walked up the yard and into the house. She wasn't kidding.

Well, I did touch the mole — at least Duke did — and lived to tell about it.

My mother took Bertie out with her, to the foot doctor or something. My job was to stay home in case the new refrigerator came. Which it did. It was huge. Green. According to my mother's orders, I switched what was left in the measly old white job — eggs, milk, olives, bacon, jelly — into the new one, and they carted the old one away. The box that the new one came in got left in the yard. Looked like a small house.

The neatest part of the new refrigerator was a spouty kind of doodad stuck right on the outside of the big green door. There was a little blue button to push.

Duke nodded, grinned. "Faucet."

"Yeah?" I said. "Like a sink?"

"Yep."

"What's it for?"

He opened the door, did some studying. "Cold water." A big grin. "*Ice* water."

"Man."

"My father seen one once. He told me."

"You mean like a watercooler?"

He just nodded. He was grinning away, a proud kind of grin, like the new refrigerator was his.

The second-neatest part was the freezer section. It was so big. Not like the shoebox in the old one. You could stick ten ice creams in this one and still have room for plenty more. Yeah . . .

When they got home, Bertie headed straight for the garbage can. Like I figured, she came tearing after me when she found out the mole was gone. She was snarling, her fist clutching a white tube of Elmer's glue.

"C'mere," I said. "Wanna show you something."

She kicked me in the shin. I grabbed her by the wrist and dragged her to the kitchen.

"Did you see the new refrigerator?" I asked, all pleasant.

She kicked me again.

I opened the freezer door. "Nice freezer, huh?" I did a quick back-step, making her foot miss this time. "Look what's on the bottom shelf there." She looked. I picked it up. It was a foot-long package in brown paper, with big red crayon lettering. "See what it says?"

She recognized her name. "Bertie!"

"That's right. I'll read the rest to you. 'BERTIE'S ZEP — DO NOT TOUCH.' "

First her face was surprised, then happy, then confused, then suspicious, then remembering. "Where's my mole?"

I waved the "zep" in front of her. "Right here."

"In there?"

"Yep."

"Lemme see."

I peeled off the tape and opened it just enough for a peek. She squealed. I rewrapped it, shoved it to the back of the bottom shelf, and shut the door.

"Why'd ya do it?" she said.

"I toldjah before, 'cause it would get all rotten. You know how meat spoils if it's not frozen."

She knew about that. Our father is a butcher.

She sneered. "That's not meat. That's a mole."

"Sure, and moles are made of meat. All animals have meat in them."

She giggled. "Mole meat."

"Yeah. And this way you can save it, and nobody'll know it's in there, because it says 'Bertie's Zep.' "

She stomped her foot. "Yeah!" She flipped the glue tube onto the kitchen table and charged out the back door.

I figured I'd sleep easy that night. But just in case, I put the glue tube in my pocket.

6

Back on the steps. The sun gone. Streetlights on.
The sounds on, too.

The sound of somebody sweeping a broom.
. . . Bingo crossing Elm, under the streetlight, passing us, heading for the park.

Every day the same thing. He comes down the
path from the park, crosses the tracks, up our street,
Oriole, three blocks to Marshall, where the stores
are. We say it's his job, but it's a joke. He just hangs
around. Then, back down Oriole, out the path to the
park for the night. Some people say he created the
path, walking it every day and night for the past fifty
years. They say he sleeps in the bandshell. They say
the only person he talks to is Maniac Magee, who's
an orphan sort of a kid, who sleeps at the bandshell

sometimes, too. Some say Bingo used to be in charge of the monkey house at the zoo. Some say he used to be mayor.

I said, Duke said, "Yo, Bingo."

His one hand went up, came back down, like a lever. It's all you ever get from him. It's automatic. "Yo, Bingo" — hand goes up, down. Never his head. His face is always down, like fifty years ago he lost something somewhere between the park and Marshall Street and he's going to keep looking for it till he finds it. About all you see from the neck up is ratty gray hair and beard.

A couple houses down, a little kid darted onto the sidewalk, bumped smack into Bingo, gasped, "Yo, Bingo," (up the arm, down) and tore across the street to a hiding place. Playing Outs.

Bingo became a shadow as he left the streetlight behind. But you could still hear him. He takes real short steps, like he's afraid he'll stub his toes, and his feet never leave the ground. They slide . . . somebody brooming.

All of a sudden, Duke jumped up and ran down to Bingo. In a couple seconds he was back.

"What was that for?" I said.

He lounged along the steps. "Gave him a quarter."

"The quarter from Mrs. Bohannon?"

"Yeah. Actually, I stuck it in his pocket."

I glared. "Great. How're we gonna save up for the Perfect Day if you go giving our money away?"

"Was only a quarter."

"Yeah, and it was half of what we had. And besides, he ain't even a beggar. He wasn't begging you. You don't *have* to give him nothing."

"Who said I had to?"

"Well, who else is giving him their money, huh? Who else?" He just sniffed and took out his knife and opened it. He propped an ankle on his knee, scrunched his foot over and started digging dirt out of the grooves in his sneaker soles, like I wasn't even talking to him. "Krymineez — okay" — I leaned back, folded my arms — "okay — Perfect Day, huh? For-get it, man, for-*get* it."

Nobody talked.

Out of the dark along the block came the calls of the little kids playing Outs.

"Seventy-eight! Seventy-nine! *Eighty!*"

"Go slower! You're counting too fast!"

"*I'm* here! Find another place!"

"Eighty-nine! *Ninety!*"

"Tell him to stop counting so fast!"

"I'm not ready!"

"Hold it! I'm switching places!"

"Ninety-four! Ninety-five!"

"Slower!"

"Ninety-eight!"

"Hold it!"

"Ninety-nine!"

"No!"

"One *hundred!* Ready or not, here I come!"

Sudden, instantaneous, black silence, like somebody clicked the volume knob off. A shadow darted noiselessly behind Dorsey's, the store across the street.

Duke said, "So, when're we gonna do the mole thing?"

"Hey," I said, "forget it, man. Who cares?"

About then Hobie Hongosh cranked up: "Naahhh! Gittaway from me! Gittaway! Stop!"

Hobie lives next door. Corner house. He's a little on the hyper side. Paranoid, too. Thinks his mother's out to get him.

"Help! No! No! Don't do it! Somebody stop her! She's beating me!"

Twice that I know of, new neighbors have called the cops, but when they came and saw which house it was, they didn't even get out of their cars.

"She's breaking my arm! Wait! No! Wait! Wait! My arrrrrmm!"

At first the hollers were coming out the first-floor windows. Now it was the second floor. "No! Not now! In a minute! Gimme one minute! Please! Pleeeeeese!"

About halfway through the "Pleeeeeese!" the sound level dropped off. Probably the bathroom door shutting. Bath time.

Funny, there's never a sound from Mrs. Hongosh. Sometimes I wonder, Is she there?

I said, "My sister goes to a class."

"Yeah?"

"Yeah. Baton twirling or something. My mother makes her."

"When?"

"Thursdays. Four o'clock."

"We do it then."

Every couple minutes a new shriek from the Outs game. The hiders being knocked off one by one.

"So," I said, "how?"

Duke pressed the main knife blade, the side of it, against the end of his nose, flattening it. He thinks that way. "We set it up in the backyard. Advertise. Charge —"

"Whose?"

"Whose what?"

"Backyard."

"Mine. Who else's? Advertise. Charge — hmm — five cents to see it?"

"Dime."

"Okay, dime a pop." He thought some more. He turned to me, grinning, the knife pointing, street light glowing in his wide eyes.

I stopped him. "Hold it — *listen* —" The Yellskis were cranking up. Two houses from the Bohannons'. I call them the Yellskis because the only part of their name that I can ever remember is the "ski" on the end.

Duke got up. "Goin' down?"

I got up. "Guess."

We moseyed on down to the curb one house away from them. Pretended to be playing Chew-the-Peg with the knife.

As usual, Mrs. Yellski was doing most of the yelling. And as usual, she was going so fast — and so loud — that we couldn't make heads or tails of it. Every once in a while a word would jump out, but it would never make sense, like: "flogger!" or "jip-tah!" or "nootch!"

I guess there's a yeller's language only fighting adults understand. Mr. Yellski seemed to. He would wait till Mrs. Yellski stopped for a breath, then he would roar: "Enhhh, *bush*wah!"

The Outs kids drifted over. Pretty soon there were eight or ten of us. After a while there was a final "*bush*wah!," a door slammed, and that was it for the night.

Back to the steps.

"So," I said, "what were you gonna say?"

"Where was I?"

"We're gonna charge ten cents. Then you were gonna say something else."

He flattened his nose with the knife blade, closed his eyes. They shot open. "Ah!" He jumped to the sidewalk, pointed the knife. "Check this out. Prairie Dog Town. Out the zoo?"

The zoo at the park.

"Yeah?"

"Natural habitat, right?"

Prairie Dog Town is all holes and tunnels in the dirt.

"*Mole* Town?"

"Nah. Only got one mole, and he's dead. But we do it natural-style."

41

"So how?"

He headed across the street, halfway to Finster-wald's, came back.

"Aquarium. My father picks up a lot of them. They're in the cellar."

I jumped up. "We fill one with dirt —"

"Dig a tunnel in it —"

"Next to the glass, so you can see —"

"Lower the mole into the tunnel —"

"Yo, Mitzi-lovers! Guess where I just was!"

The truck-horn honk of Rhino Moast. He came sailing down the Elm Street darkness on his skateboard — the "Rhinomobile" — into the streetlit intersection, veered over to us, tried to clip my toes, then Duke's, then paraded in circles out in the intersection. "Know what I did to her? I did *this*. Then I did *this*. . . ." He was gritting and grunting and snorting and shoving his arms and ramming his butt . . .

All because he knows me and Duke are both head-over-heels in love with Mitzi Luray. Mitzi lives two blocks up and a half a block over, on Haws Avenue. Her hair is so blonde it's almost white, and she's going into high school, and she's the most beautiful girl in the West End. I'd put her up against anybody in the East or North End.

"And *this* . . ." Honking, snorting.

Rhino Moast was born with a defect. One leg is six inches shorter than the other. To bring that leg down to the ground, the shoe has a six-inch-high sole on it. Like a built-in stilt. Or tree stump.

There's only one time when anybody likes Rhino Moast: if he's on your pickup football team and you're playing tackle instead of tag. If you try to tackle him low, with that stump-shoe, you might as well stick your head in front of a kicking mule. And if you try to tackle him high, he stiffs you in the eye with his finger.

Rhino is only our age, but even older kids don't mess with him.

He veered over again — "And *this!*" — did a figure-eight around me and Duke — it's the stump-shoe he pushes off with — and sailed on down Elm out of sight and, finally, out of sound: ". . . gonna get me s'more tomorra niiiii . . ."

Back to the steps. I said, "I hate that dude."

"J. D. In."

My mother at the window.

Duke whispered, "My house. Tomorrow. We'll set up the aquarium."

He took off.

The last sounds of the night came when I was in bed: the trucks and trains. It's like I almost have to be asleep to hear them out there. I pretend they're animals, jungle cats coming out at night, whining, growling, prowling. Sometimes I hear a couple box-cars clank together, and it sounds close enough to be in my backyard. But I know they're really far away. I pretend there's a high fence out there, a stockade like in *King Kong,* and as long as they're prowling on the outside and I'm inside, I'm safe.

7

Duke has a big tree in his backyard. In the tree he has a floor. No walls, no roof. So it's not a tree house, it's a tree floor. When the weather is warm, and sometimes not so warm, Duke sleeps up on the tree floor. Sometimes when I go over to his house in the morning, I remember this. Sometimes I forget.

"Doink."

The falling card clipped the side of my head and fluttered to the ground: a leaf from a baseball card tree. It landed faceup. Pete Rose. No way he was serious.

I didn't bother to look up. "Doink you," I said.

"Go ahead," he said. "Flip."

I looked up into the soles of his bare feet dangling

over the floor. "You know I don't carry my Roses around."

"So? Flip what you got."

"You're insane. You're gonna risk a Pete Rose for a" — I fished in my pocket, pulled out a card — "Wally *Backman?*"

"You got it. Flip, Dip."

I flipped. Backman landed faceup. I won.

I bent to pick up the Pete Rose. Six inches from my fingers two bare feet, ten toes, came to earth, puffing dust. I straightened up. He was grinning. He turned and headed for the house. I thought I should stop him, grab him, say, "Here, take it back. You don't know what you're doing." But I didn't. I put the Pete Rose in my pocket.

"Want breakfast?" Duke called, heading in the back door. I was halfway there when the duck got me. I hollered. By the time Duke came back out, the duck had me cornered between the duck house and the scavenger junk shed. It was flapping its wings and quacking and pecking away at my pantlegs.

Duke called: "Roscoe — halt!"

Duke thinks he's training the dumb thing — to be a search-and-destroy duck, whatever that means. Problem is, the stupid bird only attacks people it knows, including the Pickwells themselves. The little Pickwells are always plotting to assassinate it.

"Roscoe — halt!"

Peck peck peck . . .

"Roscoe — atten-*hut!*"

Peck peck peck . . .

I was doing the Irish jig. "Ain't workin', man."

Finally, he grabs the duck by the neck, and I escape into the house.

I said, when Duke came in, "Someday somebody's gonna call the cops on that thing."

"Great. When I'm done training him, I'm gonna rent him out to the police department. Imagine if you're a criminal and you see a police dog *and* a duck coming at you." He opened the refrigerator. "Waddaya say — scrapple?"

In came Doris Pickwell, grumbling, "Get outta my kitchen."

Doris is the oldest of the six Pickwell sisters. Whenever Mrs. Pickwell is working at her thrift shop, Hey Look Me Over, Doris gets to be in charge. It's gone to her head.

Duke acted like she wasn't there. He pulled out a brick of scrapple and pancake syrup.

Doris seethed: "If you think you're gonna mess this place up five minutes after I cleaned it . . ."

Duke pulled a skillet from under the sink.

Doris screeched: "I just *washed* that!" She planted herself in front of the stove.

Into the kitchen raced the twins — Dion and Deniro. (All the Pickwell kids' names start with "D." "Duke" isn't a nickname. It's his real name.) The twins were all over Doris, like mosquitoes. "Doris!

Doris! Waddaya want for your birthday! Huh? Huh? Huh?"

Doris swatted at them. "I don't *know!* Anything! Just get outta my *kitchen!* Stop *clawing* me!"

The twins zoomed out the back door, through the yard (the duck in their dust), and down Rako. They race everywhere they go. Nobody has ever seen them walk. The screen on the back door bulges out like a pregnant lady from them bashing into it.

Baby wailing in the living room. The newest Pickwell: Didi.

Doris groaned, snarled at Duke. "I'll be back here in a minute. I don't wanna see a speck of *dust* out of place, *boy.*" She walked out.

Duke whistled his way around the kitchen, pulling out some dishes here, silverware there. It kills Doris that no matter how nasty she acts, she can't tick Duke off. He dumped some stuff in my arms, got a load himself, and shouldered through the door. Ten minutes later we had our own kitchen in the backyard. The stove was a couple cinder blocks with a grate bridging them. A card table, a folding chair, and a rocker came from the scavenger shed.

The greatest smell in the world is scrapple smoking and sizzling on a skillet. I kept the fire going under the grate while Duke flipped the scrapple slices. Pretty soon the twins were back from the dump.

"Thought you were shopping for Doris," said Duke.

"We were," said one.

47

"But we smelled the smell," said the other. "Whatcha doin', Duke? Cookin' out?"

Duke said, "Yep," and waved them away. "Now git on back down there and find her a present. A nice one. I'll save you some."

The twins raced screaming back down the hill.

Fried scrapple. Crisp and crunchy on the outside, soft and mushy on the inside. Drenched in syrup. Mmmm. We ate like kings.

With an audience.

One by one the little kids were drifting over, reeled in by the scrapple smell: Hobie Hongosh, silent without his mother and smaller than his voice; Erin Bohannon, dressed in a purple body suit that she kept tugging on and couldn't figure out; Bertie; and, of course, the Pickwells — Dion and Deniro (back from shopping, with an egg-shaped silvery picture frame and the top half of a lipstick tube), Dominic, Dolly, Donald, Damaris, Deirdre, and Dawn — all except the baby and Doris, who kept snarling from the kitchen: "You're not so funny, *boy!*"

They all just stood around, sniffing, staring. With so many people to attack, the duck got confused and started pecking away at the legs of the card table.

Duke was eating every other bite. The rest he would mop in syrup and hold out on his Swiss Army fork — a kid would step forward, take the piece between his or her teeth, step back, chew, and go to heaven.

Idea!

I leaned over the table, whispered: "Hey, you got more in there?"

"More what?"

"Scrapple."

"Yeah, tons."

"Great. How about more tables? Chairs?"

He glanced back at the shed. "Yeah, prob'ly."

I leaned in closer. "Okay, listen. Let's open a restaurant. Make Perfect Day money. Waddaya say?"

He slapped the tabletop, jumped up. "Let's go!"

We rooted through the junk shed and came up with more tables and a bunch of chairs. We just had them set up when I heard my mother calling me. Most mothers, when they want their kids, they go to the door, cup their hands, and bellow. Not my mom. She'll walk to the end of the street before she'll bellow. That's how I knew this was bad.

I looked at Duke. "The mole."

He nodded, saluted. "Sayonara."

She met me halfway up the backyard. Didn't say a word, just handed me a knife. I didn't have to ask what for. I continued on through the air shaft to the sidewalk, dropped to my knees, and started gouging grass out from between the bricks. It's the punishment I hate most. My mother reserves it for the most atrocious crimes.

Two hours and two raw, aching kneecaps later, I was limping back to Duke's. In our yard Bertie was practically diving headfirst into the garbage can, yanking stuff out, stomping: "Where'd she *put* it?"

Duke's yard was back to normal, except for the duck pecking at some spilled scrapple. From the top of Rako I could see six or seven Pickwells marching single file through the stone piles, Duke leading. I went down to meet them. They were rattling. They were carrying shopping bags of dishes and utensils. One twin had an armload of sponges, the other had a giant blue box of Cheer.

Duke said they washed everything down at the creek, since Doris wouldn't let them do it in the kitchen.

"So," I said, "how'd it go? The restaurant?"

"Great," he said. "They had scrapple coming out their ears."

"How much did we make?"

"Huh?"

"What did we make? How much?" He just stared at me. His mouth worked into a smile, but it was sickly. I stepped in front of him, stopped him. "Duke, how much?"

"I forgot to charge," he said.

8

We were in the tree, sitting on a lumpy green love seat that Duke's dad had scavenged the night before.

I'd been busy the night before, too. I pulled out the piece of paper I had been working on, handed it to Duke. He settled back, slung a leg over the loveseat, and read:

PERFECT DAY

8–9 zeps (Lou's) and strawberry milk (Little Market)
9–10 Walt's Oldies
10–11 Ramjets (Dee-Dee Pizza)
11–12 Singing Bridge
12–1 water ice (Marcy's)
 1–3 movies

3–5   roller skating
5–6   zeps
6–?   Ramjets

"Well?" I said.

He nodded, handed the paper back. "Looks good. Maybe stick another strawberry milk in there."

"I'll work on it." I folded the paper, stashed it. "Now, how do we pay for it? Thanks to you, we still only got twenty-five cents. A measly quarter."

He looked surprised. "You still got it?"

"Yeah. Why not? It's for the fund, ain't it?" He just stared. "I got an envelope. It says Perfect Day Fund. Everything's gonna go in there."

With the blank face he gave me, I could have been talking Swahili.

Bertie came stomping down the alley with a brown paper Acme bag. She stopped under the tree, looked up. "Duke, can I come and live with you?"

The duck waddled over, ready to start nipping. She smacked it in the face. It waddled off.

"What's the problem?" said Duke.

"My mother won't let me make a living."

"No?"

"No. Y'know that mole I had? I was gonna put on an exbinition."

Duke smothered a giggle. "That so?"

"Yeah. It was in the freezer and she stold it."

"No!"

"Yeah. And I can't find it."

"That's too bad."

"Yeah, and that's why I'm leaving home. Can I stay with you? I could live in the tree. I could take Roscoe for walks."

Duke had to hide his face.

"Bertie," I said, "the Pickwells already have eleven kids. Why don't you go back now, and we'll talk it over later. Maybe you can sleep in my room tonight."

She wasn't listening. Not to me. She heard something else. Then I heard it. A low, deep-down rumble: heavy, throaty, like the stomach-grumble of some lurking jungle beast.

Bertie screamed, "Train!" and beat a cloud of dust down Rako Hill.

"Don't get too close!" I called.

We climbed to a higher limb. The grumble got louder, closer. It shook off all the other tinny, trafficky noises like they were fleas. It was just out of sight, beyond the Chain Street curve. I could feel it — a tremble through the tree, right through the soles of my sneaks. Little kids and dogs were pouring from the backyards, funneling down the alley, Niagara Falling down Rako Hill. Nobody even noticed Erin Bohannon streaking along with just one white sock on. And there it was — blue, boxy diesel, nosing, grumbling around the turn. Then another. Then another.

"Three engines!" shouted Duke, and we screamed,

and the little kids below screamed, and then you couldn't even hear the screaming, and for about five seconds, while the roofs of the three blue engines passed below, I knew what it was like to be swallowed by an iron monster.

The engines groaned on toward Red Hill. The tree relaxed. We were still alive. Now came the endless clackety-clacks, the little kids counting cars, squeaking higher with each number: ". . . seventy-*five!* . . . seventy-*six!* . . ."

The rusty red roof of the caboose was passing below when Duke said, "Okay, got it," and climbed back down to the love seat.

I followed. "Got what?"

"How to make money."

"How?"

"Hop the train."

"Right. Everybody knows that — hop a train and get rich."

The little kids were scampering back up the hill. Bertie and another six-year-old were leading Erin Bohannon by the hand back to her house.

Duke pointed to the shrinking caboose. "Where do you think it's going?"

"How should I know?"

"What's the biggest city around?"

"Philadelphia."

"Nah. Bigger'n that. Biggest of all."

"New York?"

He slapped my hand. "Bingo. I bet that's where that sucker's heading for. New York." He squinted at the disappearing train. "New York City."

"So?" I said.

"So." He stood up. "We hop the train, ride 'er to New York, hop off, and start selling."

"Selling? What?"

"Anything. You name it. You know my uncle Jack?"

"Nope."

"Well, he's from around there, and he says you can do all the shopping you want up there without ever going into a store." I just looked at him. "No kidding. People sell stuff out on the sidewalks. Anybody can do it. You just lay your stuff down on a blanket, right on the sidewalk, and start selling it."

"Hop a train, huh?" I had always thought about it. Who hasn't?

Duke grinned. "Yeah."

"New York."

"Umpire State Building."

"New York City."

"Come back with enough for *two* Perfect Days."

A giggle broke out. Then another. I couldn't stop them. Neither could Duke. Standing. Laughing. High fives.

"All *riiight!*"

Up to Duke's room in the attic. Rooting through the incredible mess — the dump is neater — till we find the old seabag. Scrounging around for stuff to sell. ("Like what?" "Like anything. They buy anything up there.") Finding stuff under the bed that disappeared years ago. Plastic flute. Green soldiers. Lincoln Logs. Compass. Water gun. Chopstick.

Down to the other dump, the one by the tracks. More stuff. Tennis balls. Extension cord. Fingernail clipper.

When the seabag was full, we stashed it in Duke's room and headed for the kitchen to make food for the trip. Doris growled, but she couldn't kick us out because it was lunchtime and we had a right to be there. Six sandwiches for each of us. Liverwurst and onion for Duke, peanut butter and banana for me. To drink: Kool-Aid. In a metal flying saucer-shaped canteen for me. For Duke, in the comma-shaped leather bag he calls his "goatskin."

We went down to the tracks. Walked them, Duke on one rail, me on the other.

"How do we work it?" I said.

"We just see it and hop it."

"What if we're not together? What if I'm at my house?"

"I'll come get you. I'll hear it when it's still down at Elm."

Walking the rails. Warm. Hard. Silver. Don't get wider, but seem to. Hands in pockets.

"What if it comes at night?"

"I'll hear it way off then. I'll be in the tree. I'll knock for ya."

56

He would run down to my yard, grab a clothespole, and use it to tap-tap on my bedroom window. And I would finally get to use the rope that I made last summer. The one that lies coiled in my old Matchbox car carrying case. That has a loop to go around the bedpost and is long enough and strong enough to lower me out the window and down to the ground.

I wobbled, tilted, toppled. "Man . . . just thinking about it . . . *man!*"

I climbed back on. Duke steady on his rail. "Yeah, I know. Me, too."

We came to the street that goes down through the park, that we never take the tracks past. We stood there, watching the silver rails pinching through the trees, the state hospital on the left, the creek and the park on the right, till they curved out of sight, out of Two Mills. I didn't say so, but I was sure if we just ran down to the curve — ran fast enough — and zoomed around it, we'd be able to see in the hazy distance the gray skyscrapers of New York City, maybe even hear the faint sounds of millions of people and cars.

I got the shivers.

Neither of us said a word. We turned on our rails and stood facing each other and reached out — leaning, stretching, inching — so we could slap hands without falling off. But our fingertips were still a molecule apart when we toppled and came colliding into each other. We laughed, punched a little, winged some cinders up the tracks, and walked the rails back home.

Bertie slept with me that night. She gabbed on forever, so nonstop that I never heard the rattle of the skateboard wheels, only Rhino's voice suddenly out of the night: "Yo, Kidd! I just come from Mitzi's again! Man, did we have fun! Yo, Kidd! Whatzit — past yer beddy-bye time?"

He was really close. In the alley.

"Man, whatta paira lips! Mitzi *Looo*-ray!"

Bertie wasn't even breathing. All of Two Mills was silent, cocking its ear. My face was flaming.

"*Looo*-ray! Whatta girl! Want me to tell yer pal Pigwell about her, too? Yo, Kidd!"

Squealing hinges next door, Mr. Hongosh barking: "Hey, get outta here! Go on!"

Rhino honking: "You wanna make me, horseface?"

Hinges screaming, back door slamming, running feet, clomping clubshoe, whirring skateboard wheels, laughing Rhino.

Fingertip tapping my arm. "Who's Mitzi Luray?"

"Just some girl.'

"Do you love her?"

"No way. She's just some girl lives up on Haws."

She propped herself on her elbow, looked down at me, her tiny face in moonlight. "You love her, don't you?"

"Ber-*tee* — jeez! She's going into high school. I'm in seventh. What's she gonna do with me?"

I tried to change the subject. I told her about the Perfect Day. Her answer was, "Maybe she *likes* younger men."

"Bertie, go to sleep."

"Does Rhino love her?"

"How do I know? Good night."

"Rhino kissed her. He said."

"Good for him."

"He said" — she tried to make her voice low — " 'Man, whatta paira lips!' "

I squeezed her cheeks to make a fish mouth. "Listen, shrimpo. He's just saying that. He probably didn't even see her. He's only in seventh, too. What would she want with him? Now good night."

I let her go. She opened up: "Maybe she wants a ride on his skatebuhhhh —"

I had her cheeks reclamped. "You gonna say good night?"

Her figure-eight-shaped mouth moved. "Buh-buh."

I let her go.

She said, "Good night." Two seconds later she was climbing over me to the floor. "I gotta say my prayers." She knelt by the bed.

The prayers went on for about an hour. She prayed for every relative we have, every person on the street, including Bingo, every pet, insects, planets . . . and when she said, "Please bless Mitzi Luray" for the third time, I snapped "Amen!," hoisted her into bed, stuffed her under the sheet, and fingertipped her eyelids till they stopped quivering and stayed shut by themselves. In a minute she was asleep.

I stopped praying on my knees a couple years ago. Sometimes I don't even close my eyes. I mean, in the dark, what's the point? I whipped off the standard stuff in under five seconds: "Please bless all my relatives and give us world peace." Then I asked to have what Rhino said not be true. Because I couldn't help feeling that no matter what the age difference was, Rhino could force Mitzi Luray — or just about anybody — to do anything he wanted them to.

A faraway ghost whistle moaned in the night. Boxcars clanked. Truck gears gnashed. Out beyond the stockade fence, the animals were prowling.

I wondered what I'd do if the train came on a night when Bertie was sleeping with me. I had moved the rope box from the closet to under my bed.

9

The tennis ball was on the fence post.

First thing I saw when I went out next morning. I pulled it off, headed down the alley to the telephone pole, checked to make sure nobody was looking, and opened the secret safe.

The secret safe is a boxy little space that we chiseled out of the pole, near the bottom. We leave messages there for each other. The tennis ball on the fence post signals me that there's one waiting.

I read the note:

MEET ME AROUND FRONT

I put the ball back, along with the notepad and pencil and the Elmer's glue that Bertie had threatened me with, and I closed the safe. The cover is a piece of wood that looks like pole wood and plugs the hole perfectly.

Duke was on my front steps, sprawled back.

"What's up?" I said. Then I noticed he was eating something. Liverwurst and onion. "Hey, that ain't one of the ones for the train, is it?" No answer. "Man, you used up one of the sandwiches. They're supposed to be —"

He was pointing down the street. I looked. There was a U-Haul truck in front of the Gardenhires'.

"Wow . . . moving." I sat down.

We watched. The Gardenhires lived on the other side, about halfway down. The back of the truck was facing us, so we could see everything. The whole family was working: out the door, down the steps, up the ramp, into the dark box, down the ramp, up the steps, into the house. Out loaded, back empty. Ants. The ramp stuck out like a tongue, gagging.

David Gardenhire was a year behind us, still in grade school, so we never had much to do with him. Besides, he was a sissy. He still cried. I mean, in the open, where everybody can see. That made him one of Rhino's favorite targets. Better get himself straightened out before he hits junior high.

Duke said, "Wanna mosey on down?"

I said, "Nah."

He didn't argue. People moving, you keep your distance. Unless you're little. The little kids were already there, standing, gawking.

I said, "Where you think they're moving?"

Duke just shrugged.

"North End?"

Shrug.

"Not the East End."

Shrug.

Nobody moves *from* the West End — or any end — *to* the East End. It only happens the other way around, like with our family. If you move to a new end from here, it would be the North End, where the rich people live. But most people, when they move, they move to another part of the West End, to one of those streets up the hill, like Haws or Stanbridge or Noble, or maybe even to the top of the hill, to Buttonwood, where the houses have yards in the front *and* back, and the alleys are wider.

Duke doesn't understand moving. He never lived any place except where he is, at the top of Rako Hill. He doesn't see why anybody would ever want to move. Naturally. He's got it all — the dump, the tracks, the path, the creek — right outside his back door. His tree. His knife. No wonder.

"They're moving to California."

At first I couldn't figure where the voice was coming from. Mrs. Yellski was standing there, about three doors down, looking at us; but I didn't recognize the voice, and why would she walk up from her house to say something to us?

"They're moving to California."

It was her all right, I saw her mouth move. I looked

around. Who could she be talking to? Strange, hearing her not yelling.

Duke said, "Yeah? Los Angeles?"

But she was already walking away.

We sat. Watched.

Bingo went by.

"Yo, Bingo."

Arm up, down.

MIA Rose came out — and had a problem. She lives next door to the Gardenhires, and the back end of the truck was in front of her house. Every day she comes out and sweeps. I mean *sweeps*. Not only her own sidewalk, but the sidewalks of the two houses alongside her, and then she hits the gutters of all three houses. Every day.

There she was, broom in hand, staring at the movers.

Her real name is Mrs. Rose Fortunato. She has (had?) a son, Anthony. He was in the army in the Vietnam War, like Mr. Pickwell, and now he's listed as missing-in-action. MIA. Not that I ever knew him; all this happened before I was born.

They say she painted the sign when the war ended, when every church bell in Two Mills rang and she expected him home any minute. It's about a three-by-three-foot panel of wood, and it's painted white with big red and blue letters. It says:

WELCOME HOME
ANTHONY

Except you would never know it if you didn't live here. The paint is all cracked and peeled, and the thing looks like a puzzle with half the pieces missing. It just sits there, propped up outside her cellar window. They say, at first, for a couple years, it hung over the front door. Nobody dares to touch it. Or say anything to her about it.

So, after checking the situation out, MIA Rose swept her own sidewalk, and the gutter and sidewalk of the house on the other side of her, and then she went in. But she left her broom outside.

Duke popped up. "Let's go."

"Where to?"

"The island."

"All right!"

We slapped hands and headed down the street. We ran. We raced. We didn't look at the U-Haul. Whooping. Yelling. Across the tracks, past the dump, through the stone piles, down the bank — I hopped three rocks, Duke plowed right through the water — we were there.

We went a little wild. Animal calls. Skipping stones. Pitching baseballs (round stones for fastballs, flat ones for curves) to batters (trees) on shore.

The island is about the size of, maybe, a backyard. About half is covered with grass — big blades, like steak knives. There's dirt and lots of small stones and one bush. On the other side of the stream is the armory. National Guard. We crouched behind the bush, pretended we were staking it out, waiting to attack. We lobbed grenades.

Duke sat down, pulled his soggy sneaks and socks off, rolled up his pantlegs, and stuck his feet in the water. I did, too. We laid back, hands crossed behind our heads, sky-gazing, grinning.

"This is it, man."

"Livin'."

"Where you figure the creek goes?"

"Schuylkill, I guess."

"Yeah?"

"Prob'ly."

"We oughta follow it sometime. See."

"Yeah."

"Hey, man."

"What?"

"New York City, baby!"

"Hoppin' one."

"Hoo-wee!"

We slapped feet.

"No more eating sandwiches, man. Gotta save 'em."

"Right."

"Creek still polluted, y'think?"

"Nah. There's fish in it."

"Minnies."

"So? You want whales? Hey, wanna have a contest?"

"Like what?"

"See who falls asleep first."

"You're looney, man."

"One — two — three — *go!*"

Duke won.

"Hey, idea."

"What?"

"We get sand. Bring it here. Make us our own little beach."

"Let's do it."

"Got our own ocean. Right here."

"Let's *do* it."

Feeling the ocean on our feet.

"California. You believe it?"

"Figures. They all cry out there."

Laughing. Splashing. Roaring.

When the trees from shore pulled their sheet of shadows over our faces, we picked up our stuff and took off. The front of the Gardenhires' was bare. Their sidewalk and gutter and MIA Rose's gutter were kitchen-table clean.

10

Hot. First real roaster of the summer.

Up in the tree. The shade. Playing Monopoly.

Playing Old Maid. Me always winning, because Duke can never keep a straight face when he's stuck with the old hag.

Bombarding the duck with hockers.

Flipping baseball cards. Duke not even checking his cards before flipping. Losing a Wade Boggs to me that way. Dumb. Dumb.

Talking.

About New York.

About the Perfect Day.

About Lou's zeps.

Keeping an ear cocked for the train.

Suddenly Duke gasped, "Starving." He dropped to the ground, bolted for the kitchen, duck nipping.

"Duke!" I called. "Don't do it! Don't *do* it!"

He did it. Came back with two sandwiches. One liverwurst and onion, one peanut butter and banana. And a canteen. And the goatskin.

He unwrapped his sandwich, did the thing he always does with his hand, started chomping. I just sat there. He lifted the goatskin so it was upside down in front of his face, the spout an inch from his open mouth. He squeezed the skin, and pink Kool-Aid shot into his mouth. He pulled the goatskin back and the pink stream got longer and longer, arching dead-center into his mouth. He unsqueezed — the stream cut off like a faucet. "Ahhh." He took another bite. "Ain'tcha hungry?"

I told him that was beside the point.

" 'ot if 'ou're 'ungry," he mouth-fulled.

"It's not even lunchtime."

"Snacktime."

He tossed my sandwich into my lap, the wrapping cool from the refrigerator. I threw it back.

"It's suppose to be for the train, man."

Another swig from the skin. "Ahhhh. Got plenty left."

"You got four left. You started out with six. You ate one-third of your sandwiches so far."

He chewed, swallowed. "That all?"

I snatched my sandwich and the canteen and took

them back to the refrigerator. From the tree he called: "J. D.! Get me another, will ya!"

I went home. Made my own sandwich for lunch. Went riding the rest of the day. Myself. Passed Mitzi Luray's about a hundred times.

Next day, still roasting.

When he did it again, I just glared at him for a while. Then I said, "Waddaya think, that makes it okay?"

"Huh? What?"

"That thing you do with your hand, every time you eat."

He thought. He did it: touched his forehead, then each nipple. "This?"

"Yeah."

"Crossing myself."

"Whatever."

Duke is Catholic. I'm Protestant. Presbyterian. Unless you caught me in Sunday School, you probably wouldn't know it. Nothing really shows. But Catholics, they're easier to tell. They do the hand thing — crossing themselves — all over the place. Like, before shooting a foul shot in basketball or kicking an extra point in football or trying to start up a junky car or eating. Some of them wear little oval medals around their neck. And they have strings of beads called rosaries. And they go to church on Saturday, for confession. And all that's not even counting Sunday!

"So," he said, "what's your problem?"

"I don't have a problem."

"So, what was it you said?"

"I said, it's like you think you're making it okay to eat the stuff for the train, by doing that, crossing yourself."

He took a swig from the goatskin. "That's not why I do it."

"So why?"

Another snort, a shrug. "I don't know."

"Well," I said, "it looks to me like you think you can do that and — poof — it's not wrong anymore."

He stared at the sandwich. "You mean, it's wrong to eat this?"

"Yeah," I said, "if it goes against a plan. Yeah, it's wrong."

"Does that make it a sin?"

"How should I know? I ain't God."

This wasn't going the way it ought to.

He stood up, craned. "Hey, what's going on in your yard?"

I got up, looked. Little kids were lined up at our back door.

"I don't know. Something to do with Bertie, I bet."

He finished off the sandwich, took a long snort. "Ahhhh."

"I ain't an expert," I said, "but I wouldn't be surprised if it was a sin, come to think of it. Prob'ly comes under losing control of yourself. Doing whatever you feel like. Like the Prodigal Son."

A button on threads — daddy longlegs — walking up the treetrunk. Duke took aim with the spout of the goatskin. "Maybe" — quick, hard squeeze: pink Kool-Aid laser beam, zapped spider gone, now at my feet, stilting across the platform, dignified, no sweat, like, "Hey, happens every day." Duke reached down, ramped his hand so the daddy could walk on, elevatored it back to the trunk, and let it off, higher, where it would have been if it hadn't got zapped. Finished — "it's just a Protestant sin."

I guess he believed it, because he kept eating and crossing himself, and by lunchtime the next day I was ready to blow my top.

"That's six!" I screeched, as he unwrapped the last of his sandwiches and chomped into it. "You ate every one of them!"

He just nodded, chomped away.

I couldn't stand to watch. I climbed to the next branch up and sat there. Little kids were lined up at our back door again.

The day was another roaster. Murder. No doubt anymore: it was a heat wave.

Below me, Duke arched his head back till he was looking straight up at me. He raised the goatskin over his face, spout down, squeezed — nothing came out. "Shoot, dry," he groaned.

Secretly I was glad.

A minute later he jumped up from the love seat, announced: "That's it. I can't stand it no more. I'm getting me a strawberry milk at The Little Market." He dropped to the ground, called: "Comin'?"

I dropped to the platform. "Duke, you can't. That's on the program."

"Can't help it. I gotta have it." He headed for his bike.

I jumped to the ground. The duck was on me like salt on fries. I stood still. Usually he only attacks when you're moving.

"Duke, wait!"

Duke halted, but didn't turn.

The duck was staring at my foot. "Duke, listen. You're gonna spoil it. How's it gonna be special if we start doing all the stuff on the program? We gotta save it. For the Day."

He was edging toward his bike. His hands were on the bars. I ran. The duck attacked. I ignored it. "Duke! No! You'll ruin it!"

He turned. His eyes were crazed. "I gotta."

He was wheeling the bike across the yard, the duck nipping at the pedals.

"Duke, it's like Christmas. It's no fun if you peek at your presents before the day, right?"

"I always peek. I always have fun."

"We gotta save it." He swung his leg over. I propped myself in front, braced against the handlebars. "Duke, control yourself. You don't even have any money."

"I'll carry bags at The Little Market till I get enough."

He was trying to push the bike forward. I dug in hard.

"Duke, *no!*"

"I *gotta.*"

I knew I couldn't hold him forever. I was starting to go backward.

"Okay — Duke — hold it, wait, wait — okay — wait." He stopped pushing. "Listen — *listen.* Are ya listening?" He nodded once. "Okay. Now promise me you'll wait here. I got an idea. I'm gonna let go, I'm gonna go into your house, and I'm gonna do something — if I can — and then I'm gonna come right out. Soon's I can. A minute. Okay? Will ya wait? I'm gonna take my hands off the bars — see? — okay? Now I'm gonna run to the house, and I'll be right back out, no tricks. Okay, buddy? You stayin'?" He grunted. "Promise?" He nodded.

I bolted, beat the duck to the kitchen door.

"Doris!" I gasped. "You got a blender?"

She was scrubbing the sink. She looked at me like I was talking Chinese.

I looked around, spotted one by the toaster. "Great. How about strawberries? Something strawberry?" She just stood there, working her chewing gum, like a cow. "Doris! Duke's having a fit! I need strawberries!"

She said it very slowly, very quietly. "Don't you touch a thing in my kitchen."

I ran to the fridge, yanked open the door. Strawberry . . . strawberry . . . there! Strawberry preserves. I grabbed the jar, grabbed the milk, took them to the blender. I had never used a blender before. I took the lid off, poured in some milk — about half full — dumped in two, three spoonfuls of preserves, put the lid back on, studied the row of little button cubes, nothing saying "Milk" or "Milkshake." What did I want? Puree? Blend? Liquefy? I took a breath and pressed Liquefy.

Nothing happened. Doris standing next to me, plug in her hand.

"Doris. No kidding now. Gimme that." Long past one minute.

She wouldn't. I reached. I got it. We both had it. We wrestled. Grunting. Shoving. I yanked the plug away, jammed it into the socket. She pulled my hair, screamed. I punched a button, any button — something wrong! Rattle! Clatter! Lid not on tight, flying off! Pink stuff sloshing, lashing my face, spraying the kitchen, spraying the world . . .

I pulled the plug. Pink foamy stuff still in the pitcher. How do I get the pitcher off the base? Yank, twist — it's off. Puppy? Do I hear a puppy? Doris. Staring at her wet shirt, at the walls, her mouth wide open but only making little squeaky sounds. I leaned closer: "Wha'd you say?" Nothing. Just squeaky, tiny little puppy sounds.

I tore out of the house. Duke was up to the telephone pole.

"Here! Here! Look! Strawberry milk! See?"

He stared. He didn't believe it till he curled his fingers around the wet plastic handle and tilted the pitcher to his lips and guzzled the whole thing down.

He caught his breath. He smiled. His pink mustache stretched out. He went, "Ahhhh."

We walked his bike back.

"C'mon," I said, "let's get outta here."

"Where to?" He was calm, normal.

I took the pitcher from him, set it on the kitchen step. "The island. Dip our feet in the water. Cool off." It was scary-silent in the kitchen. I pulled him. "C'mon."

We ran: Rako, tracks, dump, stone piles. Duke hit the bank first — but didn't go down, pulled up, motioned for me to be quiet. I tiptoed up to him, craned over his shoulders, through the leaves, down to the creek.

Somebody was on the island.

76

11

"It's a girl," he whispered.

"No kidding."

She was lying on a towel, on her back. Wearing a bathing suit. Pink and purple stripes. Lying at attention, arms straight by her sides, palms down. Brown bottle of suntan lotion, standing. Yellow flip-flops, one crossed over the other.

"Who is it?"

"I don't know."

She looked about our size. Her skin almost vanilla white. Her toes ended in ten bright red dots.

Duke backcrawled, ran to the nearest stone pile, grabbed a big one, came back, crouched, winged it. It plopped into the rippling water at the head of the island. The white body didn't twitch.

I whispered, "Maybe she's dead."

Duke shot me a lopsided look and ran for more stones. This time he unleashed a volley: *bam-bam-bam.* They landed all around her. She shot to a sitting position, looked around, looked right up at the weeds we were lying stomach-flat behind. We mashed our ears to the ground, heard her holler: "If that's you, Hobie, you better knock it off! Or you'll never live to see tomorrow!"

We gaped at each other, noses almost touching. Duke said it for us both: "Monica Hongosh?"

We waited, not breathing.

Monica Hongosh. Girl next door. Same grade as me and Duke, but always in the other class. Next door. Could've been Chicago, for all we ever talked. If she disappeared, I wouldn't have noticed in a year. Monica Hongosh. Bathing suit.

No more hollers. No sounds of her scraping up the bank. Minutes passed. Inch by inch our heads came up. She was back down at attention, eyes shut.

We backed off, stood, talked out loud.

"What's she doing there?"

"She can't be there."

"Who asked her?"

"It's not hers."

Duke grabbed a handful from the nearest stone pile and howitzered them to the dump.

"Let's head for the bridge," he said.

He started walking, but for some reason I couldn't move. I called: "Uh —"

He turned. "Huh?"

"Uh, listen, man, this ticks me. I'm, uh, gonna hang here a couple minutes and see if maybe I can chase her away."

He gave me a quick, screwy look and took off running. He was headed down the path to the bridge that crosses the creek; under it, where it's cool and cavey even on the hottest days.

I snuck back to the bank, squinted through the leaves and trees. What could I do to make her scram? Stones? Scary noises? Flaming sticks? A rock with a note? Saying what?

I kept figuring and figuring. And watching. Suddenly she moved — I flinched. She was turning over onto her stomach. Her legs made a V. She slid down a little, so her feet reached off the towel and her toes dipped into the water.

I tried to tell if her skin was getting darker. I couldn't. I had a nutty thought: call, Hey, you're not using your suntan lotion!

Then she was moving, getting up, picking up her stuff, water-walking the rocks. I bolted behind the nearest stone pile, watched her use a treetrunk to haul herself up and over the top. I was surprised; that bank is steep even for guys. She dropped her flip-flops, wiggled into them, looked around, pulled out the top of her bathing suit and looked down inside, picked her nose, and headed for home.

Just about a minute later, Bertie appeared at the top of Rako: "Jay Dee-eee! Din-errr!" She disappeared.

When I got to the house, ready to open the back door, the refrigerator box spoke my name. It was on its side. It almost came up to my chest.

I stooped, looked in.

"Hi, J. D."

Bertie, toward the back, sitting in the little chair from her room. TV tray. Plate of franks and beans. Glass of milk.

"Wanna come in and have dinner with me?"

I settled to my knees. "What are you doing?"

"What's it look like?"

"Here?"

"Oh" — she stabbed a baked bean; it's how she eats beans, stabbing as many as she can onto her fork — "I moved out."

"Oh, really?"

Two beans at least, stacked onto every prong, into the mouth. "Yeah."

"May I ask why?"

She put the fork down, scowled. "Because a girl can't make a living around here."

"That so?"

"Yeah. I had my own bidness, and Mommy made me stop it."

"What kind of business?"

"Selling ice water. I had lotsa customers, too."

The little kids lined up in the yard.

I started to back out. "That's life, kid."

"You're gonna have dinner with me, ain'tcha?"

"Not today. Maybe tomorra."

I turned. Something hit me in the back of the neck, stuck for a second, slid down my backbone groove. I reached back, caught it at my belt. Baked bean.

That night the train came.

I felt it long before Duke got there. Felt the low deep tremble of it in my bedsprings, far, far away, maybe down the East End, maybe way down in Conshohocken, but there, *inside* my imaginary stockade fence, coming, and when the clothespole tapped on my window, I was already stiff on my elbows, sweating, praying *Please, please,* because all of a sudden, for the first time, I knew I wasn't going to go. The eight hundred block of Oriole Street was my town. The West End was my state. Philadelphia, seventeen miles away, was another country. New York — another planet. Whatever made me think I was ready for that?

The diesel must have been around Marshall Street when I first heard it, rumbling between the black-and-white-striped gates that rise and fall like Bingo's arm, to hold the traffic back, then louder, like deep from the guttering throat of a lion, passing the trains of the Reading Line parked for the night, crossing Elm, and the clothespole popping the window now, raking it, Duke whisper-calling my name; nosing into the Chain Street curve now, coming, coming, coming, lobbing cast-iron grumbles into my room, into the space where my breath used to be — at the foot of Rako now, *here*, Duke bashing the bricks, roaring —

I ran to the bathroom, whipped on the water, flushed the toilet, mashed towels into my ears, squeezed my eyes shut. When I finally opened them, turned the water off, the night was quiet again.

12

The tennis ball was on the fence post.

I didn't even bother to check if anyone was looking. Inside the secret safe were my peanut butter and bananas, all six of them.

Later that day, as I was sitting on my front steps, Duke came pedaling by, munching on a zep. Not looking at me. A while later he came by again, this time guzzling a strawberry milk.

Other than that, he stayed away from me. Which was mutual. If he was down the creek, I'd be up in the hills. He was at the dump, I was at the park. He was at the spear field, I was on the streets.

Like that. For days.

I walked the tracks. Farther than ever before. Past

the street that goes over the bridge. Down the long straightaway, state hospital on one side, creek and park on the other, past the Legion field, the bandshell, playgrounds, dam, Boy Scout cabin, zoo, around the bend I had never seen past before, telling it to the tracks: "Jeez, wha'd he expect? Me to take off in the middle of the night? Just like that? My mother finds an empty bed in the morning?" The tracks saying nothing, not even listening. Till the trees were gone, and there were sloping hills of green and corn and two silos and a cemetery, and I thought, My God, I'm out of Two Mills!

I tried telling it to Bertie. I stopped by — stooped by — her new home. Red crayon on the front flap said 802½. Inside: rocking chair, table, toy box, Darth Vader poster, *The Fly* poster, Stop Smoking poster, a bedroll, a pillow, and Bertie, lounging on her back, arms crossed behind her head, bare legs crossed at the ankles.

One foot rose, the bottom of a bare big toe nodded twice at me.

"Good day, Mister Kidd. Are you stopping by for a visit?"

I looked closer at the toe. A little face was inked on it.

"You," I said, "got to be the world's youngest lunatic."

She popped up. "Let's have tea!" She rummaged in her toy box, came out with cups and a thermos jug. She poured. The tea was cherry Kool-Aid. She pushed one cup toward me, sat back in her rocker. "Now, let's have a chat."

I sat cross-legged in front of her. "Bertie, what would you think about somebody —"

She jumped up, hit her head — Kool-Aid sloshed, the whole place quivered. "What time is it?"

Before I could answer, she was scrambling over me and out the door. I followed her out to the sidewalk. She ran to our mail slot, pushed it open, peeped inside, screeched: "He was here!" She looked around frantically. "There!" She tore down the street, to the other side, to the mailman, who was slipping a letter into the slot at the old Gardenhire house.

Next thing, here she comes, leading the mailman by his little finger, jabbering away at him, him nodding and smiling in a dazed kind of way. She led him around back, pointed at the red 802½ on the flap. "See?"

He nodded, all serious. "I do see."

"So, when I get my letters from now on, you deliver them to my new address, okay?" To face him, she had to look straight up, smack into the sun, so she talked with her eyes squeezed shut.

He nodded. "I understand." He reached into his mail pouch, pulled out a white card. "Here you go."

She squinted at it. "What is it?"

"Change-of-address card. Fill it out and return it to me, so your mail can be forwarded properly." His eyes bounced over to me; they were grinning, but his face was straight.

Bertie hopped around the yard, waving the card and squealing. She shoved it up at me, breathless. "J. D., you fill it out, okay?"

I took it. "Okay."

She turned back to the mailman. "Can I do something?"

"Sure," he said.

She pointed at the big brown leather pouch. "Can I look inside?"

He laughed. He lifted the strap over his head and set the pouch on the ground. Bertie squatted, chin in hands, stared. She looked up. "Can I put my hand in?"

"Just don't touch the letters. They're in order."

Real slow, she dipped her hand into the pouch. Her fingertips grazed the dark, horsey inside. She went, "Ouuuu." Then she stuck her head in, all the way, and took a long, deep breath. "Mmmm."

When she came out she gave me a scrunchy, funny look. She tugged at the mailman's sleeve till he lowered himself enough for her to whisper in his ear. He laughed. He picked up the pouch and off they went.

I waited a half-minute, moseyed out front. They were heading down past the old Gardenhires'. She was riding in the pouch.

13

I checked out the island. Duke wasn't there. Monica Hongosh was.

I needed somebody. I needed to say, "I told Duke I would hop the train with him to New York, but when it came, I chickened out." And somebody to say back, "Hey, what's the big deal? So you changed your mind? So Pickwell's allowed to go taking off in the middle of the night and you're not? So he belongs to a tribe instead of a family? So what?"

I lowered myself down the bank. I crossed the stones to the island. She didn't move. She was on her stomach, her face turned away from me. This time, besides her flip-flops and suntan lotion, there was a straw-type handbag and an opened can of Orange Crush.

I just stood there like a moron. Wished I hadn't come. Wished I could leave.

Finally, after about a year, I said, "Hi."

She jerked up. Her arm flew, swiping the soda can into the water. Her boggled eyes were pure scared at first. She shaded them with her hand. They recognized me, relaxed, lowered to the ground, turned hard again.

"God! Don't *do* that."

"Sorry." I was still afraid to move.

She pulled sunglasses from the handbag, put them on, swung them up to my face. "Couldn't you see somebody's here?" The last word a silent "stupid."

I shrugged. "It's a free island."

She didn't say anything, just aimed the two dark disks of the shades up at me. After a while she gave a sneer, a snort, and went into the handbag again. She came out with a Walkman, put the phones on, tuned in a station, turned onto her back, and lay back down. With the phones and shades on, she looked like a tank commander.

I kept standing, didn't know what to do. Should I sit down? Take my shirt off? Skim stones? Say something? What? I watched the Orange Crush can go bobbing downstream and out of sight.

"Gangway!"

A crashing through the bushes on the other bank, behind the armory. Somebody coming through the leaves . . . Rhino —

"Gangway!"

Monica was sitting, reaching for the Walkman, turning the volume dial.

Rhino stood at the water's edge, feet apart, long stick in one hand, the other on his hip, handkerchief around his forehead. He pulled the handkerchief down over one eye. Sword . . . peg leg . . . Long John Silver.

"Avast there, lubbers! Ah'm comin' aboard!"

Aboard he came, a near-perfect design for creek-crossing. He only had to worry about rocks for one foot, because the other, the stump-shoe, was like a built-in rock. He just plunked it in the water — which was heat-wave-low — and the shoe on top stayed high and dry.

Monica was frozen, scared stiff, watching him. When he stepped onto the island, he reached down with the stick, lifted the phones from her head, and deposited them in her lap. He laughed. He threaded the stick through the ropy handles of her handbag, hoisted it — "Wanna see it walk the plank?" — and swung it out over the water. Monica's head followed the handbag lowering slowly toward the water; it stopped an inch away, held for a while, then the tip of a corner dipped into the water and the handbag swung back up and onto the ground. Rhino howled.

Then he turned to me.

He took one step forward, plunked the clubshoe smack on Monica's towel, looked at her, looked at

89

me, pointed the stick at me, spoke down to the top of Monica's motionless head: "You know this guy's two-timing you?"

Silence. Stillness. Water.

He poked the top of her head. "Huh?"

She cringed back, folded her legs under her, showed the jellybean bottoms of ten toes. She didn't look up. "What do you mean?"

"I mean" — pointing at me, smirking — "that there skinny dungball goes sniffing around Mitzi Luray all the time you're not looking, and then he comes around telling you you're his one-and-only lover girl." He poked her. "Waddaya thinka that, huh?"

"He doesn't tell me that."

I could hardly hear her voice. Her shoulders were hunched, like she was cold.

Rhino smacked the towel with the stick. Monica jumped. "He *don't?*" He clomped over to me, planted his face so close to mine I couldn't see it clear. "That right? You don't tell her she's your one-and-only? Huh?" Each syllable a breath-puff in my face.

I tried to speak, but my speaker was clogged. I swallowed, tried again: "No."

"Why not?"

"I don't know."

"Waddaya mean, you don't know?"

"I don't know."

Pain — on the top of my foot. Didn't look. Didn't have to. The stump-shoe bearing down.

"You like her, don'tcha?"

"I don't know."

"What'd ya say?"

Bearing down.

"I like a lot of people."

"Including her?"

"Yeah, I guess."

"Hear that?" Calling to her, still in my face. "He *likes* ya."

At "likes," a final crunch into my foot — *pain!* — then release. No answer from Monica.

Rhino's face was so close his grin was like a horizon; Monica, the East End, the world somewhere beyond it. "How many times you kiss her?"

"What?"

"How many? A hundred?"

"None, man." Whispering. "I never kissed her."

"Fifty?"

"None. Zero."

"Ten?"

"I'm *telling* ya."

The grin got pouty. "Don'tcha wanna?"

"Shoot, no. No way."

"Yo, Hongosh."

No answer.

"Hongosh!"

"Huh?" A peep.

"Know what he says? He says he never kissed ya."

"He didn't." Strong, loud.

"Know what else?"

No answer.

"Hongosh!"

"What?"

"What *else*."

"What else?"

"He says he don't even *wanna* kiss ya." To me: "You rat." The grin backed off; into view came a finger pointing at me, blurry between my eyes. "She wants you to kiss her."

"No she don't."

The fingertip tapped my nose. I hate that finger. I think he overuses it to make up for his bad foot. "Yeah she does. She's over there waiting."

"No, she ain't."

The finger was coming again, slow. I pulled my head back.

"She's drooling for it."

"C'mon, man, stop messin'."

"She wants you to give her a big wet smacker."

"Rhino."

My head was craned back as far as it would go. I couldn't retreat anymore without taking a step backward, and the water was right behind. The finger kept coming. Real slow. My back aching. No more words. Like he forgot about the kissing stuff, and now he was just grin and finger, grin and finger, coming, coming. I stepped back. The finger came on, a millimeter from my nose, not stopping until my second foot backed into the water, till the creek curled around my ankles and poured into my sneaks and made me feel like the time when I was five or six, when I peed myself empty in the middle of a sidewalk.

The finger pulled back. He howled, clomped to the middle of the island. He jammed the stick to the ground, like a flagstaff. "I hereby name this here place . . . Rhinoland!" He posed, waiting for cameras.

Monica moved. "I gotta go home. It's late." She scooped up her stuff, walked past Rhino — "Hey, where ya goin', toots?" — past me, eyes bulging. She walked right through the water, didn't bother with stepping stones.

"Hey —" Rhino called, coming, "wait — Kidd's gonna carry you over the water. Hold on!"

But she was already scrambling, slipping, sliding, clawing up the bank, her handbag flopping against her back, the handles looped over her neck. When she hit the top, I took off. Once I got about six feet up, I figured I was okay; the bank being almost vertical on that side, no way he could handle it with the stump-shoe. Not that he was interested. He was bellowing, "Yo-ho-ho and a bottle o' rum!" when I rolled over the top.

Monica was halfway up Rako and tearing.

14

Rotten.

And getting rottener.

Chickened out on the train plan. Chickened out with Rhino. Best friend gone. Perfect Day gone. Nobody to talk to.

Liar.

Coward.

Rotten kid.

I rode.

All over the West End. Past St. Francis. Wished I were Catholic. I'd go to confession on Saturday night, like Duke. Tell the priest what a rat I was. He'd say, "You're right, you *are* a rat." And for punishment make me cross myself a million times.

Catholics got it made. They never have to wait longer than Saturday night to start getting unrotted. All you have to do is follow directions. You can work it off. If you're Protestant, all you get is your mother every night as you head up the stairs: "Don't forget your prayers."

I rode through the West End to Jeffersonville. To Shrack's Corner. To the Singing Bridge. Waited for a truck, wheeled onto the iron grid, went slow, coasting, daring, hoping — then feeling it in my handlebars, truck on the bridge, charging, the grid singing higher and higher — then he sees I'm going slow, air brakes gasping, right behind me now, feeling its hot breath, its huge shadow in my peripheral vision. *Go ahead, go ahead, run me over.* But it doesn't. I sail off the bridge, still alive, holler as he passes: "I'm rotten!" He gives a friendly wave and toot and roars into Valley Forge.

I sat on Finsterwald's steps. Bertie saw me, came running, pulled, tugged, pleaded, wailed till I had to let her drag me back across the street. She made me tea in her house.

Fourth of July. I didn't buy caps, sparklers. Nothing. Usually I would spend most of the day with the Pickwells down around the dump and stone piles. Cherry bombing the rats. Launching rockets. Saluting the flag that Mr. Pickwell sticks on top of the biggest stone pile, wincing while he screeches out "Taps" on a lumpy old bugle.

The only flag I saw this time was the one hanging out from the door of the old Gardenhire place. MIA Rose, next door to them, used to have a flag out all the time, they say, like maybe it would help get Anthony home. But the flag got beat up and shredded and fell down, and she just swept it up with the dirt, and all that was left was the fading sign.

While Pickwell cherry bombs boomed down by the dump, I watched MIA Rose come out with her dustpan and broom. As usual, she swept the sidewalk and the curb and the gutter, and this time, maybe seeing's it was a holiday, she broomed halfway across the street. Funny thing, though: she swept in front of the house on the right, the Trankles', as usual, and in front of her own house, but she didn't do the new people, the ones with the flag. And she never used the dustpan. She just kept sweeping the pile of dirt along the gutter till it was in front of the new people's. And that's where she left it, a gray hill of dirt a couple inches higher than the curb — left it and took the dustpan and broom and went in.

I didn't go out to the park for the races and contests and stuff. I didn't go out for the fireworks that night. I heard them thumping and booming at the Little League field, saw them sprinkle above the trees. And somewhere in there, between the cannon boomings, I thought I heard something else — a note, high-pitched, higher than the Singing Bridge could ever reach. At first I thought it came from the fireworks, like if a single pulpy pearl of a high sprinkler, falling to earth, made a sound when it hit, this would be it.

I moseyed down the dark street toward the exploding sky. I stopped at the new people's house. It was coming from there. It was violin music. Not radio. Somebody was playing.

The windows were open. There was a glow beyond the living room, kitchen light probably. Upstairs was dark. MIA Rose's dirt pile was still there.

I went down to the end, around and up the alley behind. Lots of light back there, spilling onto the yard. The back bedroom. That's where the music was coming from.

I stayed.

And stayed.

I got the shivers.

Crazy. I mean, *violin* music?

But I couldn't move. Only when it stopped was I free to go.

I walked up the alley, smack into Duke.

He was overjoyed, patting me, punching me, pushing me. I was afraid he was going to kiss me. "Hey, man! J. D.! Where you been? I keep lookin' for ya! Man, we bombed that dump! Dominic hit a rat on the run with a cherry bomb!"

"Really?"

"Yeah. Bomb hit 'im and bounced off and exploded. Shoulda seen that rat. Where ya been?"

"Ah, y'know, around."

He looked down the alley, looked at me, grinned. "You hear it too?"

"Huh? Hear what?"

"The music."

What was he up to? "Waddaya mean?"

"The violin music. Coming from the Gardenhires' house. You didn't hear it?"

"Oh, that," I said, "yeah, I think I did hear something around there. I was just walking past."

He punched my shoulder. "Ain't it beautiful?"

Was I hearing right? Was he pulling my chain? Ready to pounce as soon as I admitted it? And *beautiful*? He never used that word in his life, not even talking about a knife or a salamander. Nobody under twenty — especially no boy — uses the word *beautiful*.

"C'mon." He grabbed my arm, pulled me back down the alley to the yard.

The music was coming again. Duke let go of me. He just stood there, his face turned up, eyes shut, silly, contented grin, like he was taking a nice long shower in the music from the bright second-story window.

When he came out of his daze, he looked at me. "Well?"

"Well what?"

"Waddaya think?"

He wasn't kidding. It was no act.

I nodded. "Yeah, not bad."

"Not *bad?*" He jerked my arm. "*Listen.*"

We listened, standing. Then sitting, right there in the alley. Not speaking. Till it stopped for good and the light went out. Even then we waited a minute, like hoping it would go back on. Then we left.

Firecrackers were still popping, here, there, in the West End night.

Duke said, "I been coming over every night."

"Yeah?"

"Yeah. To listen."

"Who's doing it?"

"I don't know. Just, about four nights ago, I was riding past. Heard it. Had to come back every night."

"Yeah," I said, "see what you mean."

When we hit the street, Duke stopped. "Hey, almost forgot." He fished something out of his pocket. "Here ya go. Made it baggin'."

He gave me a dollar bill, crumpled.

"What's this for?"

"Waddaya think? The Perfect Day. You hold it. You're a better treasurer'n me."

I folded the bill, pocketed it. "The Day's on?"

He seemed surprised. "Sure. Who says it ain't?" He slapped my back. "Hey, I got more ideas for making money. We'll make enough for a perfect *month.*"

I was going to say something, about the train and being sorry and all, but I didn't. No need.

I went home then, to bed. Feeling great. Lighter. Except for one thing that kept nagging me. A tiny little thing, but it wouldn't go away; and after a while, after the last firecracker popped and the trucks and trains came out to prowl, I got up, pulled on my jeans, snuck downstairs and out the door. Forgot something. Back in, feeling along the dark walls, furniture, got the kitchen trash basket, back out. Down the street in bare feet to the new people's house, to the dirt pile by the curb. Quick, scooped it up, about five handfuls, dumped it all in the basket, hightailed it home. Two minutes later I was asleep.

15

It was Duke's mother's idea. Go around and collect used clothes from people, and she would stick the things in her thrift shop and give us half of whatever they sold for. "It's called consignment," she said.

So we went to houses, Duke with his seabag, me with a pillowcase. We did his block of Chain Street first, dumped off the stuff we collected, and started on my block of Oriole. Duke made the pitch. He's better at talking to grown-ups.

Mrs. Hongosh, first house, was ready to give us two belts and a sweater, when Monica lurched out from behind her and snatched the sweater with a glare and a snarl: "That's mine."

Mrs. Kime, on the other side of us, gave a pair of

shoes. Mrs. Yellski gave five men's shirts, a woman's bathing suit, and a pair of earmuffs.

Mrs. Bohannon gave us a bunch of little stuff. I wondered if she was figuring that if Erin was never going to wear clothes, she might as well give them away.

Bertie and her wagon came rattling down the sidewalk. In the wagon were a stack of paper cups, a bowl of ice cubes, and a plastic pitcher of Kool-Aid.

"Whatcha doin', you guys?"

We told her.

"Can I come along and sell my Kool-Aid?"

"Why aren't you back in your new house?" I said.

She made a face. "Nobody comes to visit me, and I'm not getting any mail."

Duke said to her, "You go to City Hall?"

She gasped. "Why?"

"You gotta have a license to sell food and drinks on the street."

Her face twisted. She kicked a wagon wheel. "Aw, man."

Duke laughed for ten minutes. Bertie came with us.

Down one side of the street, up the other. Pajamas from the Zavinskis. Mittens from the Sentolas. Pants from the Bluitts. Scarves from the Sobecks.

At each stop, Bertie stuck her nose in. "Can I interest you in a nice cold cuppa Kool-Aid?" When they asked how much, she said, "I'm having a sale today. Only a nickel." I was surprised how many took her up on it — from thirst or pity, I couldn't tell.

The most unusual donation came from the Wentz house — also known as the bedfast house. Because, so we heard, there was a bedfast person on the second floor. Nobody ever saw this person, who supposedly had been up there for years.

Strange word, *bedfast.* I was Bertie's age when I first heard it, and I pictured somebody up there scooting down the hall on a bed with wheels. Then I found out it means, like, so sick or so old or so both that you can't get out of bed, can't even get one foot down onto the floor. Twelve o'clock midnight, twelve noon, dinnertime — whenever — you're there. Every second of every day. The bed your house, your block. Forever.

Some kids thought it was spooky. They figured whoever it was up there was practically a cadaver. A zombie. Not me. When I thought of the bedfast person, I pictured somebody all shriveled and wrinkled and white-haired and wearing a long white nightshirt. And the person — I figured it was Miss Wentz's mother — would be there with maybe the sheet up to her knees, maybe sitting back against a couple pillows reading a magazine or propped on one elbow doing a crossword puzzle or pasting old snapshots in a scrapbook. In fact, one way or another, she would do just about anything she wanted. It just had to be done in small doses, and slow. She wasn't really all that different from us on the outside. It was just that one day she sort of slipped back a little, into another category, and since then, she couldn't quite make it over that hump that gets you out of bed each morning. But the good part was, she didn't even especially want to.

When Miss Wentz came to the door and heard what we wanted, she didn't say anything for a long time. She just kept staring at us, blinking, twitching her mouth and nose. She clamped her lips together and sucked them in until they disappeared; finally she said, "Wait," and went back in.

She took so long, the three of us got into a whispering argument about whether or not we should go on to the next house. When she came back, her arms were piled high, and her eyes and nose were red. "Here," she sniffed, and Duke and I started lifting stuff off. There were thick woolly black pants and white shirts with yellow stains and a green sleeveless sweater with moth holes and a pair of black shoes and suspenders. Duke's eyes met mine, both of us thinking: It's a man. Her father? I wondered. Or grandfather? Whatever, right then I knew he wasn't up there cheerfully pasting up old snapshots.

When Bertie asked if she'd like a nice cold cup of Kool-Aid, she shook her head no. Then Bertie said, "Well, is there anybody you'd like to buy a nice cold cuppa Kool-Aid *for?*"

Miss Wentz blinked, staring down at the red wagon.

Her mouth went through a whole series of expressions, like it was looking for one to settle on; one of them, for an instant, was a smile. She gave a short nod. "How much?"

Bertie jumped, squeaked, went to work. "Oh, it's free for you, Miss Wentz. Each day there's a lottery, and one house on the block gets a free Kool-Aid, and today — guess what? — your house won!" Bertie plopped in an ice cube and handed Miss Wentz the cup. She beamed: "Congratulations!"

Miss Wentz looked stumped. "Why?" Then: "Oh, yes. Thank you." She took the cup and went in.

We were ready to knock at the next house, when we heard "Wait!" Miss Wentz was hurrying down the steps toward us. She put her hand on Duke's seabag. "Can I see, please?" She rummaged inside, came up with the moth-eaten old green sleeveless sweater. She clutched it to her chest, looked again into the seabag, backed off, nodded, gave a quick smile, and went back to her house.

16

We were still three doors down from the new people's house when we heard the violin music. Duke and I drifted toward it like two rats to a pied piper. Bertie hung back, squawking about skipping customers.

All of a sudden Duke got shy; he didn't want to do the knocking. Neither did I. So we both did. Waited. Nothing. Knocked louder.

The music stopped.

The door opened.

I knew why MIA Rose had left the pile of dirt.

The face was Vietnamese. On my own, I couldn't have said any more than somewhere in the Far East. But with MIA Rose, the dirt pile, the sign — it couldn't be anything but Vietnam.

Girl. About our age. Dressed American: jeans, Super Bowl XX T-shirt, bare feet. Most of all, the eyes. So big. Huge. I thought — crazy — of cookies — Oreos — the iris almost black, floating on pure white icing.

The three of us might still be there gaping at each other if Bertie hadn't barged up the steps and stuck her hand out. "Hi! Are you the new neighbor?"

The girl hesitated, nodded. "Yes?" She gave her hand to Bertie, who pumped it up and down a half-dozen times.

Bertie threw one arm up and her chest out. "Welcome to the eight-hundred block of Oriole Street. I live at eight-oh-two-and-a-half. You can't see it from here. It's right behind that house, *there.* My name is Alberta Jane Kidd, but everybody calls me Bertie. What's your name?"

It looked like it took a while for the girl to catch up to the final question; when she did she said, "I am Joy Lin."

Bertie grabbed her hand and pumped it again. "Please ta meetcha."

Joy Lin smiled — and I finally had my Fourth of July.

"Can I interest you in a nice cold cuppa Kool-Aid?" asked Bertie.

Joy nodded. "Yes, okay?"

Bertie poured a cup, handed it to her. She stood right there in the doorway and drank it. Sipped it, actually, lifting her eyebrows and smacking her lips —

redder by the sip — and going "Mmm"; and after every "Mmm" Bertie would swing her face up to us all smug and satisfied. When Joy finished, she handed down the paper cup. Bertie waved it off. "On the house."

The huge eyes blinked. The girl was baffled. She leaned out from the doorway, looked up and down the brick front of her house.

Duke smothered a chuckle. "It's a saying. It means it's free."

Joy looked at Duke, at the empty cup, frowning. Her lips formed three silent words: "on the house." A smile came creeping — "Oh" — up came the eyes — "Oh, okay" — the smile huge now, too — "Okay." She dipped her finger into the cup. "But there is a charge for the inside? The juice?"

"It ain't really juice," Bertie told her. "It's Kool-Aid. I made it myself. 'Sides, howjah like to make a deal?"

"A deal?"

"Yeah. You can have the Kool-Aid free — as many cups as you want — if I can come in and see your house. Are you Chinese?"

"Bertie!" I yelled. I smacked her shoulder.

She whirled, kicked me — "Stop it! There's nothing wrong with that. We're neighbors. I'm gonna invite her over to my house" — turned back to Joy — "Well, waddaya think? Is it a deal?"

Joy swung open the door. "A deal, yes."

Bertie parked her wagon against the steps and marched right in. Joy asked if we would like to come in, too. She didn't have to ask twice.

Someone was sitting on the floor, cross-legged, watching TV. I naturally figured it was a kid at first, but it wasn't. It was an old man, his face glued to a game show. The TV sound was off. Just pictures.

Joy stood over him. "Grandfather?" On the silent screen someone in an elephant costume was rolling a pair of giant Nerf dice with its trunk. The old man was letting out short, squeaky laughs that sounded like hiccups. I was surprised that the girl didn't call him again. She just stood there.

Finally, with the elephant draping its trunk over a new washing machine it had just won, the old man looked up.

"Grandfather" — I liked the way she said it, the last part tailing up: Grandfa*ther*. She pointed to us, and that's where I lost her, because she switched to another language, Vietnamese, I guess, and didn't let up until the final word, nodding to my sister — "Alberta . . . Bertie."

The old man gave a big grin, one front tooth missing and one gold, and nodded. Bertie took one step forward and bowed. "How 'bout a nice cold cuppa Kool-Aid?"

Joy translated. The old man laughed and said something.

"Not today," said Joy. "Maybe tomorrow." Now

she was looking at us. "I don't know your names."

Duke gave a little wave. "Duke Pickwell."

"J. D. Kidd," I said.

The old man flashed the gold tooth at each of us and turned back to the TV.

Joy led us back through the dining room to the kitchen. Bertie was sniffing everything out. The place was pretty ordinary except for one thing: the curtains. They were purple — bright, Easter egg purple, in a thin, flimsy, filmy material. A violin and bow sat on the kitchen table.

"Why don't you put your bags down?" said Joy.

Duke and I laughed and put them down. I hollered: "Bertie!"

She was into the refrigerator. I shut the door. She punched me. "I wasn't *taking* anything. I was *looking*. She said I could look. That's the deal, ain't it, Joy?"

"Yes," Joy said, "but don't fight with your brother."

Bertie stuck her tongue out at me. "We don't fight, 'cause he knows he'd lose. Nyehhhh." She went back to the fridge.

Duke said, "Your violin?"

"Yes?"

"We heard you playing."

"Oh?"

"At night, in the back alley. We listened."

"Oh." Embarrassed.

"It was beautiful."

"Oh. Thank you."

"Wonderful."

I wanted to shout: Stop it, Duke! Guys don't use those words. What's next? Lovely?

Bertie butted in. She picked up the violin. "What's this?" I cringed. Joy stiffened but stayed put. Bertie held it to her ear, shook it. Joy bit her lip.

"Bertie," I said.

"Shut up, or I'll tell her about you and Mitzi Luray." She plucked a string. "This a fiddle?"

Joy said, "It's a violin."

Bertie reached across the table for the bow; Joy snatched it up just in time.

Bertie shrugged, laid the violin down. "That's okay. I hate fiddle music anyway." Her face lit up. "Hey, Joy, wanna guide?"

"A guide? Do I need one?"

"Oh, yeah. Def 'nitely." Bertie hopped onto a chair, squatted. "You need a guide, see, 'cause you're new in the neighborhood, and you need somebody to show you where the best places are and where to watch out for and stuff."

I said, "She's trying to rip you off, Joy."

Bertie seethed. "Butt out, buster, or I'll sic Rhino on ya." Hunched and squatting on the kitchen chair, she looked like a gnome. She cupped her face in her hands, went, "Hmmmm," thinking. "Okay," she said at last. "I'm gonna give you a sample, and if you like it, you can hire me to be your guide. Okay?"

"Okay," said Joy.

Bertie leaned forward, palms on the table, gleam in her eye. "Red Hill. You never, *never* stand on Red Hill. You know why?"

"Why?"

"Because the Devil lives there. That's why it's red."

"I see," said Joy. Her lips were fighting off a smile.

"See?" said Bertie, snooting down at us. "You get tips with my sightseeing. So, you gonna hire me?"

Joy said she wasn't sure. She wondered about the price.

Bertie said only twenty-five dollars.

Me and Duke yelled, "Robber!"

Bertie said, "Shut up, let her run her own bidness"; said to Joy, "You know what haggle is?"

"Haggle?"

"Yeah, well, it's like this. My dad told me. He's my bidness adviser. Haggle means: I say a price that's so high it's ridiculous, then you say one that's so low it's ridiculous. Like, I say twenty-five dollars, and you say one penny. See? Wanna haggle?"

So they haggled. Bertie came down from twenty-five dollars, Joy came up from one cent. They met at seventeen cents.

Bertie scratched her head. "Hmm, how'd that happen? I'm s'pposed to get more'n that."

"That's what you get for being greedy," I told her. "Now get down from there. You're hogging the show."

"Joy," she squawked, "I ain't being greedy. I'm

112

just doing what they're doing. They're making money for a perfick day, and I am too. I'm gonna have my own perfick day. I'm gonna go to Dorsey's and buy five Popsicles and ten Mars bars, and I'm gonna bake a buncha brownies and eat 'em all by myself, excep' you can have some, and I'm gonna buy a TV for my new house, and I'm gonna call Damaris Pickwell a bad name and — *hey* —"

I lifted her from the chair. I was going to put her down right there, but she kept kicking and babbling on, so I hauled her away — "Joy, I was kidding! He don't like Mitzi Luray! Know who he likes? You! He told me! He *told* me!" — and out the front door.

I heard Duke say, "Play something"; then Joy was lifting the violin to her shoulder, and in a minute there was nothing but the music. It filled up something inside me, filled it to the brim and came spilling over the brim and down the sides, all through me, spilling, all the way to the ends of my fingers and the ends of my toes. The Oreo eyes would look at me and at Duke and out to the living room where the grandfather sat and cackled, and sometimes they would close, and there would be a faint smile on her lips, and it was like she had left us behind in the kitchen, behind in Two Mills, and was away in the place where the music was born.

Each time she finished, we would say play some more, and she would. When we finally had to go, the grandfather was asleep on the floor.

17

Two days later our seabag-and-pillowcase haul was on the shelves and racks and hangers and piles in Mrs. Pickwell's thrift shop, Hey Look Me Over, on Marshall Street. I know, because me and Duke were there, running the joint, because Mrs. Pickwell had gotten a hysterical phone call from Doris yelling about the other kids overrunning her kitchen. So she told Doris to tell Duke and me to ride out and watch the shop, so she could go home and kick some butt.

If all the stuff in that shop could spread out regular, it would fill up a Sears store. As it was, everything was crammed into a space the size of my bedroom. If it wasn't in somebody's house or on the curb for the trashman or in the dump, it was in Hey Look Me Over. In fact, I was sure the pogo stick I was looking over was the same one I had seen in the dump a couple days before.

I was surprised how many people came into the place. Most of them bought clothes, but not ours. Three people bought fans — two little ones and a big one, the whole stock. Somebody even tried to buy the fan that was blowing on us. It was like an oven in there. Duke was in double agony, because The Little Market, which sells his beloved strawberry milk, was sitting there only two stores away.

"Duke," I told him, "just hang in there. Any minute now our stuff'll start selling and before you know it we'll have enough for the Day. I'm telling ya, man, you'll be glad you waited. You're gonna thank me."

Finally somebody came in and started picking up our stuff. It was Miss Wentz. She didn't say anything. She went straight for the men's section and started snapping hangers and digging through piles. Her lips clamped tighter and tighter until they disappeared, and all that was left was a thin crack between her nose and chin.

She didn't stop till she went through every scrap of men's stuff, and when she finally came up to the counter, it was all there, everything she had given us from her bedfast father or grandfather. She sniffed and looked over our heads and acted like it was all perfectly normal. She stood at attention while Duke totaled up the tags. When he gave her the price, I almost choked.

"That'll be fifty cents," he said.

She flinched, blinked a couple times, looked at him. Then she fished out a dollar and in a couple seconds was out the door and crossing Marshall. She carried her own shopping bag with handles.

I didn't say anything right away. Even at Mrs. Pickwell's low prices, the stuff had to be worth $4 or $5. And Miss Wentz would have paid every cent, been glad to. And why not? She gave us the stuff, didn't she? You can't go giving away stuff in this world and expect to get it back two days later. She knew that. She expected to pay. But I knew if I said these things to Duke, he'd just shrug it off.

Mrs. Pickwell came back. She gave us the fifty cents and we took off. By the time we were a block away, I had to let it out. "Man" — I looked at the two measly quarters in my hand — "that coulda been two zeps. And maybe a couple water ices, too."

Sure enough, he just shrugged. And just about then, I had the weirdest flicker of a feeling, like up there ahead of us, on the last block of Oriole, Miss Wentz was going through her doorway with the bagful of clothes, and upstairs a bed gave a creak as an old, old man sat up for the first time in years.

18

A couple blocks of silence, then Duke all of a sudden stops and goes: "Blue Moon!"

"Huh?"

"Blue Moon. We'll get money there."

The Blue Moon Café is a beer joint. Sometimes, when people are coming out of it, they're sloppy with the money in their hands. Like, they might go to stick it in their pants pocket, but one or two bills will go fluttering down their pantleg to the ground. They keep on walking — they never know. It's always somebody coming out. Nobody ever drops money going in.

We were there in one minute flat. But we weren't the first. Bertie was there, with Joy Lin. Joy waved to us. She was standing at the curb, watching Bertie, who was walking up and down, hunched over, her eyes glued to the sidewalk. At first I thought she was after the same thing we were; but then, when she stopped and squatted and waved — "Joy! Here, I found it!" — the grisly truth dawned on me.

"Bertie, no!" I shouted. Too late. Joy was already there, bending, looking . . .

Somebody who uses that beer joint drops the biggest lungers in the world. And the grossest. If you spread one out with a broom, you could wet down the sidewalks in front of three houses. Nobody has ever seen who does it. He's known as Louie the Lunger. It's one of the world's great mysteries.

Joy was turning away, drifting toward us. Her eyes were even wider than usual. She didn't look too healthy.

"Bertie," I snarled, "what do you think you're doing?"

She was still squatting, staring. "J. D., c'mere. This is the best one *ever*."

I went over all right. I lifted her right off the ground and deposited her alongside Joy. "Now get outta here."

"I'm just showing Joy the highlights."

"Great. Take her to your little house."

"I did."

"Then take her to the dump."

"I did."

"*Bertie.*"

For once I scared her. She took Joy's hand and led her away.

We set up a stakeout point on the curb across the street from the Blue Moon. We flipped some baseball cards, played Chew-the-Peg, held a spitting contest, talked, worked out some fine points for the Perfect Day. And kept our eyes on everybody that came out of the Blue Moon.

We stayed all afternoon. A lot of people went in and out. Thirsty from the heat, I guess. But — nothing. We saw somebody drop something once. We ran over: chewing gum wrapper. But that's how it is staking out the Blue Moon — all or nothing. You almost never get small change, because if somebody drops a quarter, they usually hear it and go pick it up. But paper money, when it lands, never makes a sound. That's the beauty of dollars.

Around dinnertime I said, "We're striking out, man."

Duke wiped dirt from his knife blade, closed it. "Yeah, but it gets better at night."

I went home for dinner. Duke stayed. When I came back, he was polishing off a pickle. He loves those big, fat Jewish ones. Pickle Pickwell I call him sometimes. In fact, he had penciled one in for the Perfect Day. I asked him where he got it.

He crushed into it. Pickle juice down his chin. He nodded across the street.

"In *there?* The Blue Moon?"

"Yep."

"How?"

He shrugged. "Went in and asked for it."

That's Duke.

We staked out till dark. Nothing. Zippo. Even though twice as many people came and went.

I had to be back on my block by dark. "Gotta go," I said.

"I'm hangin'," he said. "The later the better. Around midnight it's gonna be droppin' all over the place."

He was right.

I went home, went to bed, got up the next morning, and saw the tennis ball on the fence post. And in the secret safe: eleven dollars. A ten and a one.

He was sleeping on the platform. I climbed up, shook him awake, flapped the bills in his face. "You did it, man! You did it! How'd you do it?"

He didn't even open his eyes, grogged, "After midnight. One in morning. Jackpot."

"Man!" I screeched, "We're rich! We're on our way!"

He was asleep.

I climbed back down, outran the duck, and took the money up to my room to look at it and do some figuring. Eleven dollars was five and a half apiece. That would pay for a zep, a soda, a large Marcy's Water Ice, and the movie. Or a medium popcorn instead of water ice. Or eight games of Ramjets instead of movies. And that wasn't even counting the dollar Duke had given me before, or the fifty cents so far from Hey Look Me Over, or that first quarter from Mrs. Bohannon.

Yeah, we were on our way all right.

Until my mother saw the eleven dollars.

I left it in my room, and when I came home for lunch she was waiting with two hardboiled eggs and a question: "Where'd the money come from?"

"What money?"

"On your dresser."

"*That* money?"

"Eleven dollars."

"What about it?"

"Where did it come from?"

I bit into an egg. "Well, it's for our Perfect Day." Her face was a blank. I told her all about it. She didn't speak, just nodded. "Well, that's what it's for. The Perfect Day."

She poured my milk. "Fine. That doesn't explain where it came from."

"Oh." Another bite. "You wanna know *that?*"

"If you don't mind."

"Nah, no problem." Finished the first egg, finished the second, long swig of milk. "We found it."

"Where?"

"On the street."

"Where?"

"Huh?"

"Where?"

I knew it was coming to that. I was flipping through some lies in my mind when she supplied the answer herself: "Blue Moon." I didn't say anything. "Am I right?"

"Yeah, I guess."

"Take it back."

"*What!*"

"It's not yours. Take it back."

I yelled. I hollered. Didn't do any good. I said that by keeping the eleven dollars I was helping to fight alcoholism. She said it was a form of stealing.

When I told Duke, he winced but didn't say anything. He pressed the side of his knife blade against his nose.

I said, "Duke, we gotta have that eleven bucks."

He nodded. A couple minutes later he lifted the blade from his nose. "Wha'd she say, your mother?"

"She said to take it back."

He pointed the blade tip at me. "That's what she said? *Take* it back?"

"Yeah, take it back."

He closed the knife, grinned. "Okay. You got it?"

I forked over the money. "What're you gonna do?"

He stuffed the money in his pocket. "Tell you tomorrow."

Next day he told me. He looked a little bleary-eyed. "You said your mom said *take* it back, right? Not *give* it back. So that's what I did. I took it back.

I put the bills right where I found them, on the sidewalk in front of the Blue Moon. Then I waited. Exactly eleven minutes. One minute for each dollar. Anybody that came along coulda seen 'em, picked 'em up. But nobody did. So I did. I figure that makes it ours."

What a story! I got the shivers.

"So," I said, "You got the money?"

He yawned. "Nope."

"No? Waddaya mean?"

"It's hid."

I didn't like this. "Duke, you hid it? So you're the only one knows where it is? So you can dip into it if you get a little thirsty for a strawberry milk some day?"

He crossed himself, glanced at the sky. "No, honest, I swear. It's not even where I can get at it. Not easy, anyway. See, look" — he yawned — "this way, if your mom asks if you took the money back you can say yeah, and it'll be true. If she says is it gone, you can say yeah, it's gone, you don't have it."

Made pretty good sense. Not that I had much choice.

But something was bothering me. The chance he took laying the money on the sidewalk. People walking. How did they miss it?

"Duke," I said, "when did you do all that, drop the money back there?"

"Four o'clock in the morning." He yawned.

123

19

On the steps.

Hot.

Fighting thirst with a couple tall, cold ones, compliments of the ice water bar in our new refrigerator.

Flipping baseball cards.

Bouncing a tennis ball against the wall.

Lobbing hockers. Over the wavy brick sidewalk, over the curb, out to the street. Power not enough. Height, that's the secret. Wet white mortar shells.

Licking the cold dew on the outside of the glasses.

Bingo shufflebrooms by. Late today. Heat slowing him down, but he's still in bundles.

"Yo, Bingo."

"Yo, Bingo."

Arm cranks up, down.

Arm cranks up, down.

Erin Bohannon, bathtub-naked, darts to the sidewalk, hops in the air three times, dashes down the street.

MIA Rose out to sweep. Does the sidewalk of the house on her right. Then her own. Then the gutters. Sweeps it all in front of the Lins'. Sweeping to the sound of the violin music that flows like syrup from the windows next door. Vietnam. Vietmom. Back inside the dead house, past the old sign, hardly readable. WELCOME HOME ANTHONY.

Bertie's red wagon outside the Lins'. Every day now. With her inside. Near the music.

Across the street Finsterwald's dark green shades hang like limp tongues, the house hot, panting, like a dog.

A race. Up from the dead end: the twins, Dion and Deniro, and Erin Bohannon, dashing. Erin with them for five or six parked cars, then flying apart, laughing, too much fun to race, peeling off, the twins sprinting all the way to Dorsey's, not stopping or even slowing at the steps or even the screen door — *slam! bam!* — hear them collide with the candy counter inside.

The Lins' door opens. Bertie. Takes the toy snow shovel from her wagon, sidefoots the dirt pile onto it, dumps it in the wagon, goes back inside. She's taken over the job since I told her what was happening.

Heat snakes dance above the street.

Duke turned his empty glass upside down over his laid-back face. A single drop fell to his nose. He jerked to his feet, crazed eyes fixed on Dorsey's: "Gotta have a Pops —"

He never finished the cold, icy, tongue-staining word — a shriek pierced the screen door of Dorsey's. Oriole Street shot to attention.

Duke was halfway there before I got off the steps, was there with the twins jabbering up at him by the time I got inside.

"This big!"

"*This* big!"

"He was there!"

"And *there!*"

"He went down the steps!"

"He's in the cellar!"

"Can we go down, Duke? Huh?"

"Please Duke please oh please!"

Duke looked at me. "Rat."

The street-splitting shriek had come from Dion and Deniro together. And it hadn't been a shriek of horror, it had been delight. They were yapping and pawing at Duke like a couple of puppies. It took him five minutes and two nickels to herd them out of the store.

Miss Dorsey was behind the counter. She has short, curly black hair and fat arms with dimples where the elbows go and long yellow fangy toenails. The other one, Mrs. Dorsey, was somewhere behind the cur-

126

tain that blocks off the rest of the place. She has white hair and a pink scalp and is made of sticks and spit and weighs about thirty-two pounds and is three hundred years old. Her veins look like blue worms under her skin. You feel yourself getting ancient if she's there alone and has to wait on you. Seems funny for her to be a Mrs.

Duke said to Miss Dorsey, "Y'know, me and J. D. are going into business now. Handymen, sort of. If you'd like us to go down after that rat and get ridda him for you, we'd just charge you" — he glanced at me — "one Popsicle apiece?"

Miss Dorsey took a toothpick from her apron pocket, dug out the groove between every pair of teeth in her mouth, wiped it off, and stuck it back in the pocket. She reached into the cellar doorway, flipped on the light. "Be my guest," she said.

Duke led the way. By the time we got to the cellar floor, the boxes towered in mountains. A maze of pathways. Rat's eye view of the world. Lima beans. Pickles. Cheerios. Catsup. Creamed corn. A roach. Another. Deeper into the boxways. Creeping. Creepy. Wanting to grab Duke's hand, squeeze it like little five-year-old J. D.

I whispered, "Rat's gone, man. He ain't here."

"Shhh."

"What if you find it? How you gonna kill it?"

"Maybe we'll luck out, find one already dead. Prob'ly lots down here."

So we creeped and snooped through the maze, looking for some kind of rat.

I whispered, "Duke, waddaya think? Ten roaches equal to a rat? That be worth two Pops?"

Duke halted, thought. "Twenty maybe."

That's when the scream came, second of the morning. And this time I knew right away who it was. I whirled, headed back. But which way? Which path? I kept taking the wrong one. First I ran into the heater, then a wall. Now there was thumping overhead. Loud thumping. Finally, the stairs. I flew up. "Bertie!"

She was on top of the ice cream freezer, four fingers in her mouth, goggle-eyed. Joy was beside her. And a rat — the same one? different one? — scootered along the floorboard inches ahead of Rhino Moast's lumber foot, and because the front door hadn't shut all the way, motored on outside.

Stupid rat. It should have headed for the Dorseys' backyard or a drainpipe or under a car. But what's it do? It dawdles along the front wall of the store, and that's where Rhino picks up the attack. Clomping, stamping, he herds the rat into the corner where the front wall meets the steps. At first the rat tries to go this way, then that way. Then it's going in circles, like some windup toy out of control. Then it wedges itself into the corner, and Rhino is stamping and huffing and grunting "Yeah! — Yeah!" More screaming. I look up. Bertie and Joy are on the top step, but their gaping mouths are stone mute. It's the rat. The rat is screaming. For his cousins in the dump?

Duke says, "Rhino."

I put out my arm, not knowing why. The rat is reared up, like it wants to duke it out, screaming at the unstoppable shoe stump. And then — flop — it's dead, the scream lopped as neat as a slice of salami.

What happened then didn't make any sense. Rhino picked up the dead rat by the tail and held it up to Joy. He dangled it and swung it in front of her eyes, and his face was all proud and happy. But something was different. The smirk wasn't there. Something else was, something softer, and it was all pouring upward to Joy, and he was going, "I got him for ya. I saved ya."

Joy didn't flinch, not even with the rat ticktocking in front of her. Her face didn't cringe, didn't smile, didn't do anything. Then she took Bertie by the hand and led her down the steps. Rhino shifted in front of them. He was sweating like a hog. I never saw him smile like that. "Ain'tcha glad? I saved ya."

Joy pulled Bertie around him and headed down the sidewalk. Rhino screeched. "Hey! I killed him for ya! Hey!"

They kept walking, Bertie turning around, Joy not seeming to hear.

"Hey!"

Walking.

Rhino's face changed, back to Rhino. "Chink!" he yelled, and whipped the dead rat at them. It glanced off Joy's shoulder and flopped into the gutter. Bertie lunged for him, but she couldn't get out of Joy's grip. She snarled, tried to pry Joy's fingers from her hand, but Joy just kept walking, never turning, dragging Bertie along.

Then Duke was shoving Rhino, hand-jamming his chest and sending him backward. Look out, Duke, I thought. But Rhino just laughed, foot-flipped his skateboard up to his hand, shoved me and Duke out of the way, dropped the board to the street, pushed off to the corner, and went rattling and howling down Elm.

Thunder rumbled over the West End.

20

When it finally rained, it didn't mess around. All afternoon. All night. Half the next day.

Each gutter was a river. The gutters poured into the sewers, the sewers into the Schuylkill, the Schuylkill . . .

When it stopped, the kids came out, but they were second to the worms. The little kids were all bare feet and screams and underwear. They found the puddles and stomped and splashed and pretended to swim.

Except for Bertie. Her cardboard house was demolished. Soggy. Sagging. Collapsed. Kaput. Because the roof was caved in, she couldn't even crawl in to get her stuff out, so I had to rip through the roof and lay 802½ Oriole Street out like an open-faced sandwich. Bertie whimpered, sniveled, her lower lip out like a second blue tongue. Joy hugged her, stroked her head. Joy gave me a poor-little-kid smile, but her Oreo eyes were gleaming with tears.

We helped Bertie take her furniture inside. Then Joy led her away while I ripped up the rest of the box and stacked the pieces next to the trash can.

I went down to Duke's. What a sight. They already had a bathtub-size hole in the dirt yard that they filled up with water sometimes for Roscoe the duck. Now it was filled with rainwater, and not only was Roscoe in it — so were Erin Bohannon and one of the twins, both bare as billiard balls. Then the other twin, also naked, comes bolting from the house — Doris clutching the baby and screaming, "Come back here! Come *back* here!" — and he's got a box in his hand, and when he reaches the "tub" he turns the box upside down and showers the whole place with white powder till the box is empty. Then he jumps in.

It's bubble bath. In a couple seconds you can hardly see anything for the suds. A chunk of foam shoots out with a quack — it's Roscoe — and waddles across the yard shedding suds. The three little kids are in bubblesuds heaven.

A yell from below. Dominic and Damaris Pickwell at the foot of Rako, calling us, waving wild-eyed. We ran down. "What?"

"C'mere! Quick!"

They ran across the tracks, toward where the woods begin between the path and the creek, toward the swamp. We followed, and ten feet into the woods, we saw.

The swamp is about the size of a living room rug, a small one. It has a couple reedy stalks growing out of it; other than that it's — well — swampy. Everybody knows to steer clear of it. According to legend, a mass murderer escaped from the state hospital, and nobody could find him, till a week later somebody spotted a finger sticking up out of the swamp. The guy was supposed to be six feet tall, and figure two more feet for the upraised arm — that's how come the legend says the swamp is at least eight feet to the bottom.

But the legend is wrong, because Rhino was only in up to his ankles, or maybe a little above. He was just a step or two into the swamp, and he had one leg, the good-footed one, hauled up on dry land. The stump-shoe, that was the problem. The whole stump part was sunk into the mud, and so was the shoe part up to the knot on the laces. Rhino pulled and pulled, but the stump-shoe wouldn't come out. And that meant Rhino wasn't coming out.

He was like a trapped animal. Snarling. Spitting. Yelling. Cursing. And most of it was aimed at Bertie, who was standing with Joy about five feet away and inching slowly backward. A couple other kids — little ones, wet and muddy from puddle-playing — kept farther away, gawking, wonder-mouthed. From the sound of the yelps in the distance, more were heading down Oriole and Rako.

I asked Bertie what was going on. She said she hated Rhino ever since he threw the rat at Joy, and when she saw his skateboard parked outside Dorsey's, she picked it up and heaved it into Finsterwald's backyard. Rhino chased her, and this was what happened.

Rhino lunged and lurched and slashed and bellowed, and every time he bellowed, the growing herd of little kids flinched backward. Then he noticed me. He stopped struggling. An evil sneer slithered across his face. He aimed his single finger at me, closing one eye behind it like it was a gun. "You're the one's gonna pay, Kidd. You're gonna pay for your little sister."

Bertie barked: "He ain't payin' for nothin'! You got a problem, you come and see *me,* blimpo!"

The little kids laughed. Rhino kept his sneer aimed at me. "You ain't gonna live long enough to see seventh grade, Kidd."

"*You* ain't gonna live long enough to get outta that *mud!*" zingoed Bertie.

Little kids roaring.

The sneer left. All teeth and snarl now. "You're dead meat, Kidd. You're history."

Bertie darted forward, scooped up some mud,

shaped it into a ball, and winged it right into Rhino's chest. "Don't *say* that to my brother!"

"You're a slabba meat hangin' on a meathook, Kidd."

"Stop it!"

"A bloody, drippy, gory slabba meat."

"Shut up, you fat pig!"

Bertie was scooping and slinging mud at him without taking time to make balls. At first Rhino tried dodging, twisting, contorting around his anchored leg; then he started scooping mud and slinging it back. Bertie took one right in the puss but kept on firing. Then one of the twins came flying out of nowhere — all skin and soapsuds — and landed — *plop!* — sitting down in the middle of the slop. That signaled Erin and the other twin to cannonball their bodies into the goo, and they were all whipping mud at each other, and the kids on the sideline were peeing themselves with laughter.

With all that, I hardly heard Duke gasp, "Oh, my God." He was gone, weaving through the trees, heading for the creek.

I didn't know what to do. Follow Duke? Stay? Dion and Deniro and Erin were brown now, but they had no problem; they were too little and too light to get stuck. They kept crawling out of the muck and diving back in. Bertie was firing away at Rhino but keeping her distance. And Rhino, with that trapped shoe, wasn't going anywhere.

So I took off.

I caught up to Duke at the bottom of the bank at the island — except the island was just a little circle of pebbles about the size of a trash can lid. Stony Creek was a thousand gutters; was a churning, slathering river of chocolate. It covered all the stepping rocks. And there was Duke, wading through the chocolate, up to his knees, fighting off the tree limbs that came cartwheeling into him. When he reached the circle of pebbles, he dropped to all fours and started scooping up the pebbles, then the dirt beneath the water, frantically scooping.

He went on like that for about ten minutes before he finally gave up, slumping, and headed for the bank.

"Man," I said, "you have a hemorrhage or something? What are ya doing?"

He sagged in front of me, wagged his head. He kicked the boiling water. He looked up at me, dripping, panting. "Money's gone. Eleven dollars. I buried it. On the island."

21

When we got back to the swamp, everybody was gone. But not every thing. There in the mud, as stuck as ever, was Rhino's lumber-stump-shoe. The top was flared open and the shoelace was gone.

At home, Bertie told me the whole gruesome tale. How Rhino finally went into a wounded bull rage. How he bellowed and tore the lace out of his shoe and pulled his bad foot — except, said Bertie, it wasn't really a foot — out of the shoe and let out a roar, and all the kids screamed and ran, and he took off after them, clomping and jerking and lurching up Oriole like a peg-leg pirate.

"You shoulda seen it, J. D.," she kept saying. "You shoulda seen it."

Five houses down, Erin Bohannon was still screaming.

Bertie came over, straddled herself on my knee. She looked hard at me. "J. D., you stay away from him, y'hear?" She was more serious than I'd ever seen her.

"What do I gotta worry about?" I tickled her. She laughed and squirmed, then went stony again. "I didn't do nothing."

I knew there was stuff she wasn't saying, just behind her eyes. Stuff that Rhino had said. About me. About getting me. But I didn't want to hear it, and she didn't want to say it.

She dismounted. She wound up her leg for a killer kick, but when her foot landed on my shin I hardly felt it. "I'm tellin' ya," she jabbed, and walked off.

The next couple days I spent mostly hanging around Duke's. I didn't go on the street too much. When I did, there always seemed to be a couple little kids about ten steps behind me. They were nervous and excited. Hyenas waiting for the kill.

Kids kept streaming to the dead end. They came down Oriole, Elm, Rako Hill, the alleys, along the tracks. Kids I never saw before. From all over the West End. Heading for the swamp. The shoe. Just to see it.

It only lasted one day. By the second morning, the shoe was gone.

I felt safest up in Duke's tree. By the day after

the grim discovery on the island, Duke was back to his old self, like it never happened. Ticked me off a little. I thought he should have felt bad at least one more day. The better he felt, the worse I felt.

"So," I said, "now what? We're broke again."

He pulled tiny scissors from his Swiss Army knife and started clipping the hair on his forearm. "We ain't broke."

True, technically. His mother had just given us $1.15 from sales of our stuff. Add that to the $1.75 we already had . . .

"Duke, we got a grand total of two dollars and ninety cents. That won't even get us up to nine o'clock on the Perfect Day."

He shrugged. "We'll think of something."

That's pretty much what we did for the next couple days — thought. We thought about carrying bags at the Acme. About collecting bottles from the streets and park and dump and selling them to the recycling place. About going to the creek for nightcrawlers and selling them to people fishing down at the dam across the Schuylkill. I reminded him about Monica Hongosh in her bathing suit on the island, and we thought about luring her back there and taking a sneak picture of her and either bribing her to buy it from us or charging other kids a dime apiece to see it, or both. We thought about our early idea, the zoo. And about a yard sale and a newspaper route and buying raw peanuts and roasting and selling them.

One night we went scavenging with Mr. Pickwell. In the Norh End, where the rich people live. We figured we'd find a lot of expensive junk and resell it in the West End.

Mr. Pickwell also wanted us to keep an eye out for camping stuff. It was getting time for the Pickwells' yearly "return to the wilderness," as Mr. Pickwell calls it. Every summer the whole family dresses up like soldiers and mountain people and hikes off to camp — on the hills. Which are about two spits from their house.

We told Duke's dad about our ideas. He nodded. Said they were pretty good ideas, for a couple of greenhorn scouts. Said he'd try to come up with some more for us.

For camping we found a hibachi and two plastic buckets. For ourselves, nothing. There's better trash in the West End. The only difference I could see, the houses in the North End aren't all stuck together in rows, like on my street. And they're not all brick.

So we kept thinking, and Duke kept clipping his peach fuzz. He did both arms, one leg, and was down to the knee on the other when Rhino showed up. Stump-shoe on. Under the tree.

Roscoe waddled over, took a few pecks at the shoe, and waddled away.

"Okay, Kidd — down."

What surprised me, he didn't look especially mean. Not snarling or loud. And not sneery, laughy. Businessy, that's what. Almost bored.

140

"I'm waiting, Kidd."

Funny thing, I almost wished he were snarling. This way, it was like I was about to be squashed by some piece of machinery on an assembly line. Nothing I could do about it. Not run. Not plead. Not holler. Not even cry.

Rhino said, "Now, Kidd, I ain't got all day," and as soon as I started to move, Duke jumped in front of me. He had one foot on the ladder before I could stop him.

"Where you going?" I said.

He shrugged. "Down."

"What for?"

"I don't know. I need a reason?"

My eyes were stinging. Little kids were heading down the alley, stopping three backyards away.

I pulled on him. "You ain't goin'."

"Lemme go."

"No," I said — I yelled, "you let *me* go!" He was staring, wide-eyed. My throat was going into spasms, but the words were barging through anyway. "I'm tireda you being my bodyguard. Tireda my little sister . . . That's it. No more. He wants to beat the crap outta me, fine. I ain't running. I don't care if he kills me. *I'm* going down."

He let me pull him back up. I climbed down. I rubbed my tears away on the flaky bark of the tree. By the time I hit the ground, I had my throat under control.

I walked over to him. I was ready to die.

A little leer crept onto his lips. He said, "You gonna go get it?"

He meant the skateboard. From Finsterwald's yard, where Bertie had heaved it.

"No," I said.

He came closer. "Second time. You gonna get it?"

"No."

Closer. Into my face. He had been eating licorice. "Last time, bathing beauty. You gonna get it?" The stump-shoe was mashing my foot. The hated finger was pressing the tip of my nose upward. It was going to rip me bigger nostrils.

"No," I said.

Suddenly my foot was free. My nose was free. He was backing off. He was letting me go!

And then he hit me.

In the face. My right eye and the right side of my nose. My first thought was: So *that's* what it's like to get punched. My next thought was: How did I get here? I was on my back in the "bathtub" that Erin Bohannon and the twins had bubbled in after the big rain.

My third thought was: Ouch!

My eye was thumping like a heart. Blood was rolling from my nose. Somewhere, someone — Bertie — was screeching: "I'm coming, J. D.! I'll gettim!" And Duke was flying from the leaves, crash-landing on Rhino, and they were rolling and wrestling in the dust, and Roscoe was going bananas flapping and quacking. But I didn't care about any of that. It figured I ought to be feeling rotten, but I wasn't. I was feeling great. Never better in my life. Because the blood running out of my nose was following something else that had already left me, something that had been with me for a long time, too long: fear.

Suddenly the wrestling stopped. They were both staring — where? — at Joy. She was holding something. The skateboard.

Rhino shoved Duke away and lumbered to his feet. He stared at her. Nobody moved, not even the duck. Joy held it by a single wheel. Finally, Rhino clomped over. She held it out. He took it. If he said thank you or anything, it was too soft for me to hear. He just took it and went clomping on down the hill.

Bertie came running, wiped the blood away with her dirty hands. She tried to comfort me. She thought I was crying at first. Then she realized, no, I was laughing. Laughing and laughing. Her face was a riot — total befuddlement. She couldn't figure me out. Nobody could.

22

Before he pulled out for some East End scavenging, Mr. Pickwell called from his pickup. "Got your answer."

"What?" we called.

"World's Fair."

"Huh?"

"Do all the things you talked about. Why pick one? Do 'em all. Right here. World's Fair." He took off. "Think big!"

We tried it, thinking big.

"He means, like, a zoo *and* . . ."

"A nightcrawler sale."

"*And* a yard sale."

"*And* a peanut sale."

"*And* — what else?"

"Bake sale?"

"Bake sale. What else? Name it."

"Uh . . . games. Amusements."

"You got it. Go."

"Uh . . . rides."

"Go."

"Uh . . . reader. Y'know, adviser. Fortune-teller."

"Go, go."

"Animals. Pet show. Uh, crafts. Face-painting."

"Go!"

"Hot dogs! Pizza! Soda! Rides! I said that! Contests! Races! Talent show! Clowns!"

"World's Fair!"

"We're rich!"

Getting ready took about two weeks. We worked day and night. Two hunting expeditions. The haul: twelve nightcrawlers, five garter snakes, big black snake (species unknown), two box turtles, six crawfish, ten salamanders (seven all-gray, three yellow-striped), a toad, a praying mantis, and a crippled sparrow.

We made a million signs. Put them on telephone poles all over the West End. Asked people to bring baked goods and yard sale stuff and crafts.

Mr. Pickwell made booths for games and found a colossal pot for cooking hot dogs. For the contests and races, Mrs. Pickwell brought first-place prizes from Hey Look Me Over. Me and Duke got second- and third-place prizes from the dump.

We went to every food store in the West End and got them to donate pizza sauce and cheese and English muffins (homemade pizzas), hot dogs, and soda. We measured off the race course in the alley. Mr. Pickwell got rolls of change from the bank.

We did a zillion things. And still weren't finished.

But, ready or not, the day came. A Wednesday: 10 A.M. to 4 P.M.

By 10:30 the place was mobbed. The whole West End was there.

By noon we were out of pizza. Then hot dogs.

Nobody cared. Everybody was having too much fun. Roscoe went crazy, so many legs to nip at. The fair spilled over into the street in front of the Pickwells', up and down the alley, down Rako to the dump. Everywhere but the kitchen, which Doris guarded.

Dion and Deniro won the little kids' race, in a tie.

Bertie insisted on being the fortune-teller. She wrapped a dish towel around her head, gazed into Mr. Pickwell's bowling ball, and told everybody they were going to get rich.

The zoo was a big hit. We had it in a sort of tent, a sheet propped up. The customers came in one end, out the other, like a carnival side show. We had animals in buckets, boxes, fish bowls, you name it. We sold the worms for a quarter apiece. They went like the pizzas.

Deirdre Pickwell, who's fourteen and artistic, did the face-painting. Every time I looked, there was a line five kids deep at her table. Erin Bohannon had all her clothes on when she plunked down her quarter. Deirdre did her face; then, instead of leaving, Erin whipped her clothes off and squeaked, "Now the resta me!" Deirdre made a fish face on her stomach, with her belly button as the mouth, and two happy faces on her little white buns. I told Deirdre no more freebies — somebody wants a body job, it's extra.

Joy helped a lot. For a while, she ran the darts-and-balloons game. Then she disappeared, and when I spotted her again she was at Deirdre's table. Only she wasn't there to get herself painted. She had MIA Rose's WELCOME HOME ANTHONY sign.

Ever since MIA Rose had started sweeping dirt over to Joy's house, I had felt bad for Joy. So she was from Vietnam, that didn't make it her fault that Anthony was missing in action. My way of dealing with it had been to assign Bertie to scoop up the dirt pile each day, try to keep Joy from finding out that her neighbor didn't like her.

Which was dumb. How could Joy not find out, not feel it, sooner or later? And now, I saw, she had made up her own way of dealing.

When Deirdre was through painting, the sign looked brand new. Mothers gathered around to watch and applauded when Deirdre held it up. Joy was embarrassed. She had to go through a gauntlet of pats on the back before she could trot away with the sign.

Just about then, Duke had one of the great brain-storms of all time. We took all the animals out of the sheet-tent zoo and left them in the open. "Zoo's free now!" we announced. I took off for Joy's. By the time we got back with the violin, Duke had a folding chair inside the tent and a sign on the outside:

SEE THE GIRL
WHO WENT INTO
FINSTERWALD'S YARD
AND LIVED TO TELL
ABOUT IT!!!
25¢

Joy thought it was funny, but she didn't agree to do it till we lowered the price to ten cents.

So there was the scene: a million people mobbing around — running, shouting, colliding, shrieking, cheering — World's Fairing — and rising out of a white-sheeted rectangular tent, a sweetness of violin music that seemed to belong anyplace but there. But the people, mothers and kids, were lined up all the way back to the big tree waiting to get in. Joy was by far the biggest hit of the day.

Maybe if she hadn't been such a big hit, maybe if nobody had come, we would have pulled the sign down and brought the animals back in, and the accident never would have happened.

But it did.

23

The pet show was the last big event of the day. Duke was getting Roscoe ready. I had just stashed a cole slaw container of money under Duke's bed. That made four containers.

"I can taste that zep," I said.

Duke licked his lips. "That strawberry milk is half-way to my stomach."

"Marcy's."

"Yeah."

"Ramjets."

"A *hundred* games."

"Duke."

"Huh?"

"Duke" — I got a chill at the thought — "you know something?"

"What?"

"We *might* have more than we can spend in one day."

We stared at each other for a minute.

Duke said it first: "A Perfect *Week!*"

"Yahoo!"

The two pet show categories were Most Original and Best Trained. Three mothers were judges.

Most Original went to Alleyway Enfield. For a minute. Then somebody discovered that the big black snake he was holding belonged in the empty yellow bucket in the zoo. So they gave the prize to some kid from up on Buttonwood. He had a chameleon that ate a cricket and changed colors right in front of the judges.

The trouble came during the Best Trained competition. Six dogs and a duck.

Duke was commanding Roscoe to *Halt!* and *March!* and *Eyes Right!* but all the duck wanted to do was attack. I felt bad for Duke, so I walked away — checked out the games.

Later, when I heard the screams, I didn't think anything of it. There had been screams all day. It was all the barking and quacking that made me turn. A dog was loose. Big black dog, trailing a leash. And Roscoe. They were a kind of black-and-white cyclone blur swirling around and around the yard, couldn't tell who was chasing who, the mob bunching up here, parting there, little painted faces shrieking out in all directions. Then the dog was galloping full-speed into the white tent, and the sheets were falling in, billowing down, and in a couple seconds, what you had was something that looked like a hysterical ten-headed ghost.

Pretty soon everybody was laughing. The sheets were flying off, except for one that went quacking across the yard, smacked into the tree, into a game booth, then went quacking down Rako. The people in the tent picked themselves up, laughing, little by little unshambling the whole mess. Even Joy, for the first time I ever saw, didn't just smile but laughed out loud. And then somebody gasped and pointed, and people closed in, and Joy was looking down at the ground, her laugh gone, her Oreo eyes enormous. The violin was in two pieces. One piece looked like it had been left in the middle of a busy street.

24

Oh, I felt rotten all right. From the very first second. I guarantee, nobody there felt any rottener than me. Before Joy finished picking up the pieces, I was thinking up ways to help her get a new one. Like catching and selling more nightcrawlers. Or donating our Hey Look Me Over profits. Just because I didn't think about forking over every cent we made at our World's Fair didn't mean I didn't feel rotten or want to help. But when I saw Duke's face, how he looked at her, at the busted violin, and then at me, I knew without him saying a word that that's what he wanted to do. And it wasn't even that he wanted to do it that bothered me the most. It was that he didn't even stop to think about it.

Neither of us said a word. The fair ended, the people cleared out, and that night we counted our money. I relaxed. I felt better. A hundred and seventeen dollars and thirty-five cents.

I beat Duke to the punch. "Why don't we use some of this to get Joy a new violin?"

Duke just nodded and shrugged, like the whole idea was no gigantic deal to him.

And he acted the same way next morning, when he said, "New violin costs two hundred dollars."

I almost fell out of the tree. "Two *hundred?*"

"Yep."

"Says who?"

"My father asked around."

"Well, y'know, she don't have to have the best kind, a kid don't."

"Two hundred's a cheap one."

For a long time, neither of us said anything. The only sound was his knife whittling away on a stick, whittling our Perfect Day down to nothing.

I said, "What are they, poor? Poverty-stricken? Can't buy their own kid a musical instrument?"

"Not for two hundred bucks."

"Maybe she could get a loaner from school."

"Maybe she couldn't take it home."

"Maybe she could take up something else, doesn't cost so much. How about a flute? What's a flute cost?"

He didn't answer.

"Hey," I said, "wanna flip? I'll flip you my Pete Roses. 'Kay?"

He shook his head, went on whittling.

"Your big chance, man. I might not want to risk it for another year."

"Thanks, anyway," he said.

I ripped a tab of bark off the tree. "I don't believe you, man. All summer long you been wanting this. I mean, it was *your* idea, man. You sucked me into it. All summer long you been going crazy for your strawberry milk. Now you can have gallons — everything you ever wanted. You're gonna throw it all away? That what you're saying?"

He gazed out over the dump, the creek, the park, shaving wood. "I can't do nothin'. It has to be the two of us."

We sat there, talkless, in the tree, till the stick was a toothpick. He put it in his mouth and started on another. I climbed down and went home.

Later, after dinner, Bertie came to me in my room. "Duke wants to know what your answer is, yes or no. Yes or no what, J. D.?"

"Tell him I don't care!" I yelled. "Tell him do what he wants!" I snatched my pillow and whipped it across the room. It knocked my Cherokee Indian spear off the wall. Bertie didn't hang around.

Next day the tennis ball was on the fence post. I didn't bother to look in the secret safe.

Bertie came around. "Duke says to meet him at

his house so the two of you can take it over. Take *what* over, J. D.? Where?"

"Tell him I'm sick today. Tell him to take it himself."

"You ain't sick, J. D."

I reached for the pillow.

"Okay, okay."

Next day I was on my steps. Counting my baseball cards. Reading comics. Drinking soda. MIA Rose was sweeping. She took care of the Lins' sidewalk and gutter. She scooped up the dirt and carried it in. The repainted sign was so clear, I could read it from where I was.

Joy's front door opened. She was coming out. I buried my face in a comic. From the corner of my eye, I could see her cross the street, head up the sidewalk. My front door was against my back. All I had to do was reach up, open it, roll inside. Disappear. But I couldn't. I could hear her footsteps now. I nailed my eyes to the page, the inky colors. Bare feet, a pair of legs, blue shorts in front of me, at the bottom step. Waiting. No words. Finally, I had to look up. The Oreo eyes were watery, gleaming. You could swim in them. She smiled. "Thank you, J. D." She came up the steps, bent, and kissed me on my cheek. Her long black hair made a curtain that shut out the rest of the world.

25

When I went to the Pickwells' for the camping trip, I found out I wasn't the only outsider invited. Joy was there, too. And her new violin. Mr. Pickwell had gone to her house and practically begged her parents to let her come along. He spoke some Vietnamese to them, Duke said, which probably turned the tide.

As we all stepped up to get backpacks and other stuff to carry, Mr. Pickwell kept jabbering to Joy about the violin and music composers and all. It didn't seem to fit: an old soldier knowing about violin music.

It took us an hour to get all packed up and ready. Like we were heading up the Amazon for a year.

Fifteen of us — thirteen Pickwells plus me and Joy — trooping out of the house ("On to the wilderness!" Mr. Pickwell called), a line so long that when Mr. Pickwell was at the bottom of Rako Hill, Mrs. Pickwell was still at the top.

Up the tracks . . . through the hills . . . into the spear field. We were there in five minutes.

Another hour to unpack and put up tents and make a fire. We ate hot dogs and chili and toasted marshmallows, and the sky was bloodworm red through the spears, and Mr. Pickwell told stories. They were about Vietnam, but they weren't about war. They were about rice paddies and water buffalo and mostly about people in the villages he came to.

About kids, all kinds — like one who had a pet duck, and a crippled kid with no shoe for his bad foot, and a pair of twins, and a little girl — hundreds of little girls — running around without any clothes.

And a man and wife who were always yelling at each other.

And a lady who took care of her bedfast father.

And a lady who swept the dirt in front of her house every morning.

And a house that none of the village kids would dare go near.

And two best friends who stayed up in a tree house a lot.

It was totally dark when Joy started playing, except for the fire and the fireflies and the stars and the moon and the green-glowing Captain Nemo watches of Dion and Deniro. Joy closed her eyes and swayed and her arm made moving shadows against the fire-lit spear plants behind her.

After a while, the music and the campfire seemed the same thing. Now crackling and misting, now leaping, now rolling lazy-like over the logs . . . and then it was inside me, like a furry pet, only closer, curling, nestling into me . . .

All the little Pickwells were asleep. The fireflies were dancing to the music. The fire was embering, dying, like the summer . . .

What made me do it? I don't know. I only know I couldn't hold all the music. Neither could the fire or the campsite or the spear field. It wasn't my music. I didn't play it. I didn't make it. It wasn't mine to give away. And yet, that's just what I wanted to do — had to do. Give it away. Share it.

I was up, asking Mr. Pickwell for his flashlight, stopping the music, leading Joy and Duke, wondering if I was crazy, out of the firelight, through the tall moon-tipped spears, down and up a gulley and onto the bald, round top where I always ran but never stood.

"This is Red Hill," I told Joy.

"Devil's s'pposed to live here," said Duke.

Joy cocked her head and held still, like a robin listening for worms. She shook her head, smiled. "I don't hear him."

158

Below, the tracks were twin ribbons of silver flying in two directions from the West End.

I said, "Could you play now? Right here?"

I figured she would look at me goofy, but she didn't. She understood. She tucked the violin under her chin and started stroking the bow, and the music that came out spilled down Red Hill and rode the silver rails, past the dead end, the dump, the alleys, on through the West End, the East End, Conshohocken, the world. Which, right then, from the top of Red Hill, didn't seem all that big. I had a feeling that everything was a lot closer to the West End than people thought. Like, once the music rode through Conshy, another five minutes, and it would be sailing through, maybe, China, and then Africa, the jungles of Vietnam — maybe Anthony would hear, become unmissing — and maybe, another couple minutes after that, if we listened good, we'd hear the music coming down the tracks from the other direction, past Prairie Dog Town at the zoo, past Bingo sleeping at the bandshell, back to Red Hill — a silver train of music around the world!

Duke propped his arm on my shoulder. I didn't turn, because tears were rolling down my face.

"Well, dude," he said, "we'll just do the Perfect Day next summer."

"*Next* summer?" I creaked. "Shoot, man, what's there to wait for? This is about as perfect as it gets."